*f*P

THE BOY
ON THE BUS

~

A Novel

Deborah Schupack

THE FREE PRESS
New York   London   Toronto
Sydney   Singapore

*f*P

THE FREE PRESS
A Division of Simon & Schuster Inc.
1230 Avenue of the Americas
New York, NY 10020

THE FREE PRESS and colophon are
trademarks of Simon & Schuster, Inc.

Manufactured in the United States of America

ISBN 0-7432-4220-3

For my parents, my sisters, and my grandmother

1

THIS RITUAL, her son coming home from school, was all wrong. It was taking too long, and now the driver was coming around the bus.

She gave a half wave from the front door. "Everything all right?" she called. "What, Sandy? What is it?"

She pulled her cardigan tighter around her and hurried down the short slate path.

Sandy Tadaveski looked over his shoulder at the bus.

"What?" she said, pushing by him. "Charlie?" she said. "Charlie!"

Meg boarded and could see instantly and with great relief that he was alive and well in the back of the bus. A sense of *right now, young man* shot through her, setting her expression, her stance. He perked up but did not leave his seat.

"Hon?" Meg started to walk down the aisle but slowed almost immediately, each step smaller than the one before.

As he shifted from distant to close, she slowed to a stop. This was not her son.

He looked quite a bit like Charlie, on the slight side for eight, with copper hair and tea-brown eyes. But there were differences: eyes narrower, more discerning than Charlie's; curls tending to kink rather than fluff; a finer nose; skin more shiny than powdery, and filling with freckles. All told, a more mature face. Fuller, firmer, more grown into itself than Charlie Carroll's pale, tentative baby face.

"Hi," the boy said, clearly delighted with her presence. He showed no sign of being home, no sign of rising, dutifully and well rehearsed, and walking directly to the front door.

She took two more steps. He looked so much like Charlie. Under ordinary circumstances, it would be their similarities that were remarkable. Now, of course, it was their differences.

She wanted to touch his face; touch seemed the only path to sense. Separated from him by half a bus, she instead gripped the top of a seat, massaging it like a shoulder. The celled green vinyl, worn and warm, felt like skin.

"Hon? Charlie?" She spoke softly. "Chappy?"

He nodded at the nickname, then, like any boy with his own mother, turned his attention out the window. His eye lit on a goose in the side yard. "There it is again!" he said. "I wonder what its name is."

When a goose began appearing on the property a few weeks ago, Charlie had asked if he could name it like a pet. His mother had explained that wild animals are not ours to keep and that, furthermore, the goose he saw around the backyard might not even be the same one all the time.

"It should probably be called something," he said to himself, thumping the seat as though to call up memory. "Something."

"Meg?" Sandy had gotten back on the bus.

"Whose idea was this, Sandy?" she said quickly, before turning to face him.

"Sometimes the route takes a little longer in mud season," he began. "But otherwise, today was the same as every other Thursday afternoon. Thirteen times we stopped, flashed the lights, halted cars if there were any, let kids run across the road to their houses. We got one horn today, one driver in a hurry. Mostly, it seems, drivers are happy to be good citizens, to make life safer for the children."

She looked from Sandy's story to the boy, to Sandy again. She waved a bent arm in front of her, like a windshield wiper. *Start over, move on. Clear the air.*

"Then we got here—last stop—and, well, this," Sandy said. He gestured to the back of the bus.

Meg instead looked ahead, into the overwide rearview mirror, row after empty row collapsed into two dimensions. She saw what Sandy must have seen when he first stopped here, the boy sitting alone in the last seat, consumed by what he was looking at, tracing an outline on the window.

She took a few steps forward, toward Sandy, although with the trick of the mirror she was also moving closer to the boy.

"What did you do?" she asked Sandy.

"I walked down the aisle, just like you did. And I said, 'Charlie?'"

Meg turned back to the boy, in living color and three dimensions.

"'Charlie?'" Now Sandy was reenacting, raising his voice to fill the present.

The boy looked up, cocking his head at the question. Not quite yes, not quite no. As though he were being addressed by a version of his name that he was not used to, or a surname instead of a first name.

"'Getting out here?'" Sandy said, still reenacting, his words more a for-the-record accounting than a question to be answered.

"Here?" the boy said, surveying out the window.

"That's just what he did the first time I asked," Sandy said to Meg. "Said 'here?' and looked out the window like that."

Sandy himself looked from window to window, as if trying to site something properly through slats. "There's something about your place," he said, "something that makes it seem like a place everyone could have, or should have, come from."

All Sandy knew was the shape of the white farmhouse, low and rambling, with its charcoal shutters and maroon front door and, halfway across the yard, an old vertical-board barn, the size of a one-car garage. She had never asked him inside, although neither had she counted on there being enough privacy outside.

"Is that real?" the boy asked. He hit the window with the heel of his hand, and the goose shook itself, water drawing its feathers to spines. It looked like the goose was answering him, shaking its head *no*, but by shaking its head at all it was actually answering *yes*.

"Used to be something else out there," Sandy said. "When we first got here, he was looking out the window at something else."

"Just tell me," she said. She could stand no more variables, no *something else*.

"You," Sandy said. "At the front door. I kind of scolded him—'Your mother'—and then we looked back out the window and there you were, reappearing at the front door when you had been standing there only a second ago. Like a film that gets stuck showing the same frame over and over."

Meg could see it: the mother appearing . . . the mother appearing . . . the mother . . .

"I'm going to leave you two alone," Sandy said and left the bus without having stepped beyond the painted white safety stripe in front.

Meg sat in the row in front of him, facing forward. He seemed to be a good boy—*whoever he was*—and eager to please. He had fielded every question: Nothing much at school today. No, he was not cold with his jacket unzipped. The hot lunch was tuna melt. Fine, a little salty, but he liked salt.

She quickly ran out of small questions and could not yet ask the large ones, not folded like this, safe for now, her knees against the seat in front of her. She did her best to envision a world, childish but at the same time defensible, in the topography of the seatback between her knees. She concentrated as if her life in *this* world depended on it. She imagined a forest—not very clever, she knew, since the school-bus green made the suggestion with a heavy hand. But she was pleased with the exactness of what she read in the vinyl's bumpy texture: puffs of treetops as seen from a medium distance.

She slid lower in the seat. She felt ground down, could not face the craggy intricacies of another world. She had no idea how he felt. Her mind struggled even to picture him (she would not look). She recalled this boy's argyle sweater, new to her, white- and black-threaded into shades of gray, more like something a man would wear. He might be taller than Charlie, or it might be that he was more patient.

"I made cookies this afternoon," she said, although she hadn't.

She had used cookies before as bait or balm—but by promising that she *would* make them, not lying that she already *had*.

"Chocolate chip?"

He sounded like Charlie, but a mother's mind can play tricks. If she needed to, she could extrapolate. The top of a head aisles over in the grocery store could be Jeff, even though he'd been out of town for most of the past year, and she couldn't remember when they'd last been in a grocery store together. If ever. A girl's petulant "Come on, Ma" could be Katie, even though she was away at private school. Coughing, anytime and anywhere, could be Charlie.

"No, we didn't have chips," she said, still not facing him. "Plain."

She felt him squinting at her back to get her attention. "That's okay," he said. "I like plain cookies. Remember?"

She turned around. Refracted through a meniscus of tears, he was another generation removed from familiarity. She blinked him kaleidoscopic.

"Colored sugar on top?" he tried.

She could see it in how she was seeing, the multicolored, large-granuled sugar he meant—something she never would have used, never would have had in the house. "No," she managed. "No sugar on top."

"That's okay." He shrugged, dismissing his fancy hopes. His sweater hitched at his collar.

She had to look away again.

"Colored sugar is just for decoration," he went on. "I'm sure they taste good."

"Thank you," she whispered, in case this was the scale of grace for them from now on.

She wouldn't look outside anymore, either. Dusk had gathered, as had a few neighbors, the school bus standing in their midst well past three o'clock. Debbie Palazzo had jogged past and doubled back. Her husband, Vince, probably on his way home from work, had left his car a respectful distance up the road and milled back to the bus, as had Leah Gheary. The elderly Cosgroves must have been on their twice-daily constitutional and stopped to see what the crowd was about. And, of course, Joan Shearer was here. Hers was the only house in sight of the Landry-Carrolls', and she was always on the lookout.

A breeze? A changing of the guards, sun and moon? Something was checkering the sky in lighter and darker shades of dusk. Each time a band of light opened, Meg seemed to make out a voice.

—Is he armed or something?

The question deflated her. How bad a parent would she have to be to raise an armed eight-year-old in Birchwood, Vermont? *Whoever he was*. Her mind dragged this behind its every thought, like a banner behind a light plane.

"Well, are you?" It flew out of her mouth when she turned to him.

He reached up under his sweater. She had forgotten, even in this short time, that he was perfectly able to initiate action. With a flourish, he took a ballpoint pen from his chest pocket. "Ta-da," he said, waving it in the air. He clicked the retractable point playfully, in mock menace.

"I'll give you exactly five seconds to tell me what is going on," she said through clenched teeth. She couldn't raise her voice, not with Sandy and the neighbors right outside, so she rose herself, kneeled backward on the seat.

The boy slumped, making himself small in her shadow. "It's a pen," he said.

She grabbed it from him, threw it up the aisle. It made one angry pinprick of a noise and skidded under a seat.

He followed it with his eyes. "It has green ink," he said sadly. He went to go after it. Rather, he started to get up, but she clamped a hand on his shoulder. She felt her fingers catch in the ball-and-socket of his joint and drew her hand away sharply.

"That's okay," he said, rubbing his shoulder. "There's cartilage in there. It protects you. We learned about it in health class. There are all kinds of things in your body that protect you." He recited some: skin, hair, fat, a very advanced nervous system.

—The father's never home.

—And the boy's sick a lot.

—He's the long-suffering silent type, that one.

—The daughter's the real firecracker.

"Do you hear people talking?" Meg asked. "Do you care what they're saying?"

"Do *you*?"

As if he had touch-tagged her, she moved across the aisle, the seat next to him. She settled into an L, her back against the window, legs stretched past the short double seat.

Perhaps like this, her feet dangling and her surety in question, *she* was the one who looked wrong. A mother who's a little off today, who has let go of the reins. Who naps in the afternoon, or lets a child stay home from school day after day. Who can sit through an entire dinner with him, an entire dinner, without saying a word. A mother who doesn't know what to do half the time, and who, in an effort to make him better, sometimes makes him worse.

"Do you really want to know?" she said.

He nodded provisionally, wanting, she could tell, to answer correctly.

"All right then." She shifted to the edge of the seat, feet on the floor, a proper strain to her back; she would fix herself-as-a-mother there, in the pull between her shoulders, in the grown-up lock of her jaw. "I do care what other people are saying, but not because I care what they think. It's just that sometimes what other people say shows a truth you cannot see yourself. Because you're always too close to your own life."

"Am I too close to my own life?" he asked.

"You," she said, "could stand to be a little closer."

In the dark, his teeth looked phosphorous, his smile Cheshire.

Heavy footsteps at the front of the bus. Meg felt a sense of impending rescue.

"Folks." Sheriff Handke, in winter-issue law-enforcement boots.

"Ben," Meg said.

"Hi," the boy said.

"What's the problem?"

"Oh, Ben." What else could she say? *This isn't my son. This is not Charlie.* Surely the sheriff would have to write up something like that, enter it into some kind of permanent record.

Ben rotated his shoulders as if to crank down his neck. He was too tall for a school bus. He turned to the boy.

"Everything okay here, son?"

"Yes," he said.

Nothing more. Meg hoped that in the presence of the sheriff, the suction of silence would draw something out of the boy, as she'd bet it could in petty crimes, shoplifting or running a red light. When consequences are in sight, guilt can get the better of people.

Meg waited for a confession, an explanation—for *anything*, really, even for Ben to articulate the question, to say, *What's your name, son?*—but the guiltless boy matched the adults in silence, measure for measure.

Finally Ben said, "Shouldn't you two go inside?"

"In my house? Just him and me?"

Meg stood up and, with her body, backed Ben Handke to the front of the bus. "It's hard, Ben," she said.

She wanted to go on: *He knows things. He knows things Charlie knows. He knows there's always too much sodium in the school's hot lunch. He knows about this goose he wanted to name. He knows to stay on my good side, if he can find it.*

"I know, Meg," Ben said. "But we've all got to go somewhere. And soon. It's against town ordinance to have the school bus operating outside its designated route hours."

That was the best Ben could do—an *ordinance*, nomenclature of traffic and leash laws and zoning—when an entire child was gone? Unless Ben was making this up, marking time until he could figure out the next move.

She wanted to back the sheriff, the sentinel, right off the bus and keep walking. To the house, where she would wait for Charlie. Wait better, wait harder. She would go to his bedroom and check his equipment, the nebulizer, the inhaler, the materials he used for breathing exercises. She would make him a special meal that was high in protein *and* tasted good. She would go to the stairway and study the framed pictures, Charlie and Katie descending in age as the steps ascended.

No, she wouldn't either. More variables. It was entirely possible that she would never see again the son who picked at his eggs or cereal or protein toast in the morning before his mother took the plate away, knowing she was nourishing him all wrong. The son who spent most of his time in his room practicing his breathing or doing word searches, or who stood outside in the yard waiting for that goose when his mother insisted, finally, that he get some fresh air for a change.

Ben Handke stamped his feet, one then the other. Meg felt this in her own legs. The body of the bus connected them—the boy, too—as surely as an electric circuit.

"Well, I'll leave you two for a minute," Ben said, "but let's not take too much longer."

He climbed down the steps, footfalls palpable the length of the aisle. He stepped off the bus. Connection was lost.

The sheriff was a big man. Meg feared the school bus would levitate without him.

It did not. The bus did not lift off the ground. She did not find herself and the boy hovering above the house, asked to take celestial stock of what lay below. *Well, that's one thing to be grateful for*, she thought.

·   ·   ·

She heard Ben report, "Domestic situation, folks. Nothing to be concerned about."

—Domestic situation? That's plenty to be concerned about.

This was said kindly, with understanding. A man's voice, must be Vince Palazzo, followed by kind, nervous laughter.

Meg could hear Ben and Sandy talking but couldn't make out what they were saying until Sandy raised his voice—not in anger, not Sandy. Rather, so she could hear him, she surmised.

"I *know* them," Sandy was saying, a trace of pride in his voice, if Meg wasn't mistaken. "They're very good with each other."

If it would bring back her Charlie, Meg thought in a silent bargain with a rarely invoked God, she could fall for Sandy Tadaveski.

Since Jeff started traveling all the time, Sandy had taken to watching her in the morning as the bus waited for Charlie. She might be carrying firewood into the house, shoveling the sidewalk, or checking the plug on the car's block heater. She could see him watching her; he was not the least bit coy about it. The mornings Charlie wasn't going to school, she could have just waved Sandy on, but she often went out to the bus. And he waited until she was safely back inside before driving on.

He lingered in the afternoon, too. More and more, Meg went out to meet him, the two of them standing on a patch of changing ground, snow, ice, snow, mud, ice, mud. When she stomped her Sorels or clapped her down gloves against the cold, he leaned toward her a little, breathing in what she had been cooking—bread, stew, mulled cider for Charlie. Sandy must have thought the nourishing scents emanated directly from her, when really it was that the coats and gloves hung just outside the kitchen. She envied him this image—wouldn't that be a nice thing to believe?—and the last time he leaned into her, she let him kiss her.

—Why don't they go inside?

This was the self-satisfied voice of Joan Shearer, whose sons wore their pants too high. Patrick and Douglas, or Tron One and Tron Two, as kids called them. They were no doubt at home right now doing their schoolwork. They were hours off the bus, the stop before Charlie's, their place a quarter mile away but distantly visible, pushing right up against the road, as if the house itself were nosy.

This boy—whoever he was—wore his jeans belted at the hip, where they belonged. For a moment, she saw him not as Charlie, nor as not-Charlie, but as himself, this boy in particular.

"Should you come in?" Meg said.

His face went reflectional. *Should he? He would have to ask her, his mother.*

—What's she afraid of?

Joan Shearer again. *Afraid of?* This from a woman who had never learned to drive, who was in thrall to her sons, and who had taken for a husband the famously dull (not to mention tiny) Allen Shearer.

"Are you afraid?" the boy asked.

"Afraid? No, of course not," Meg said, and said quickly.

Brimming with headache, she stood, knowing he would too.

Yes, he was taller. He dipped his chin, looking surprised by, or shy of, his height.

She walked up the aisle as slowly as she had walked down it hours earlier.

Outside, people, neighbors, stirred with attention.

Sandy Tadaveski approached Meg and held out his bus driver's jacket, a fleece-lined windbreaker. "It's gotten colder," he said, nodding to the moon-metal sky.

Meg took the jacket as openly as she could bear, letting Sandy feel a transfer of warmth. She started to put it on. "Oh," she said, turning around. She struggled it right off and offered it to the boy. He shook his head. Of course. He wore a lined windbreaker of his own. He was, after all, dressed for school—good boy—for a bus ride, for the outdoors. It was only she, who had intended to peek out the front door and get right back to preparing dinner—dinner! he must be hungry—who was coatless.

Joan Shearer piped up, "Is everything all right?" Her perfect question: kind on the surface but cruel just beneath.

"Everything's *fine*," Meg said. She sank her hands into the windbreaker pockets, warmed and pilled by Sandy, and instinctively drew her fingers into fists.

"Meg." Ben Handke approached her. "Jeff's on his way."

"What? He's all the way in—"

"Standard operating procedure. As the boy's father, we had to notify him."

"What, exactly, did you notify him *of*, Ben?"

"Listen," he said. "The last thing I want to do is get involved in a family's business. But when it comes to two fully custodial parents, I have my marching orders. Both parents need to be notified any time law enforcement is contacted."

Meg turned to the boy. "Did you hear that?" she said. "Did you hear who's coming?"

"All the way from—?"

"Yes, all the way from Toronto."

"To see me?" In his long-necked eagerness he seemed like a flightless bird.

"I'm sure."

"Oh. I wish he was coming to see you."

"I don't suppose there'll be any way around that. Try as he might."

Ben Handke and Sandy Tadaveski stood head to head, conferring. When they broke from their huddle, it was clear that Ben was in charge of the crowd, Sandy in charge of Meg and the boy.

Ben's job was the easier. "Folks," he said.

The ruly, small-town crowd dispersed quickly, trailing plumes of relief. They had evenings to get on with, families to feed, babies to put to bed, houses to clean.

"Meg . . ." Sandy said.

She closed the second-to-top snap on the windbreaker, which smelled of mint and sawdust or cedar, a coolness incongruous with its flannelly warmth.

Sandy looked to the boy, but said nothing. The silence landed as a slight, rather than the awkwardness it clearly was. *Say something to him,* Meg willed both herself and Sandy. *Rescue him.*

"I need to get the bus off the road," Sandy said. He gave a mock salute. "Sheriff's orders."

"Where do you go after me?" the boy asked.

Sandy laughed nervously, then tightened with embarrassment.

"I've always wondered where you go after the last stop."

"To the district lot behind the School Department. That's where I park the bus."

"Then you get it from there tomorrow?" asked the boy.

Meg's knees weakened. Oh, God, *tomorrow.* Her front door, some ten yards from the road, seemed prohibitively distant. No lights burned at the house—it had been afternoon when she stepped outside for a moment. There was a vegetable stew that had been on the stove too long, although it was on such a low heat that it posed no real danger, except perhaps to itself. She found herself equating light with heat, the house's total darkness with the winter's bottomless cold, even though they were already surfacing toward spring, toward thaw.

She had lied to the boy, she realized, had promised him homemade cookies, had told him she wasn't afraid, because she never thought that he would remain extant long enough to come inside.

"Sandy," she blurted, "don't come tomorrow." The boy looked stricken. "Jeff will be here," she said. "The whole thing. Really, Sandy, the whole thing."

"But Mom, *school*."

"Don't call me that." She grabbed his arm. That very advanced nervous system he was so sure of kicked in now. She could feel it gunning his heart, telling his synapses in no uncertain terms to pull away. But he didn't move.

Nor did she. His live weight felt so similar to Charlie's, as if the mass of her son were all here, just shuffled around some.

"Should I . . . ," Sandy stammered. Although he wouldn't look at Meg clutching that arm, he was as good as staring. "I really should . . ."

He walked away, apology in his gait.

Meg let go. The boy stood a little taller and seemed to lighten some, leavening like a good bread dough. Full night closed in behind the departing bus. Mother and boy, together alone. No bus driver, suddenly, no sheriff, no neighbors. No family. Not even the spine-feathered goose, which might or might not be the same one all the time.

2

IT WAS FOUR-THIRTY in the morning when headlights swept across the front of the house like breath on eyelashes. The beams did not change the quality of the light inside; nothing could add to this light, every bulb burning. Meg sat waiting in the living room.

The headlights shone next to the house for a good long time, pooling into the side yard like water for a skating pond. The engine's hum could have been a pump's. Jeff must have been steeling himself for home.

The boy had sent himself to bed right after dinner. It had been quite late. He had easily eaten two helpings of the thick-skinned stew and probably would have eaten more, but Meg thought the consistency was all wrong and stopped dishing it out. Charlie would use food mostly as cover, waiting for something else to happen during a meal. Conversation. He would look at his mother until she looked back, then his eyes would shoot down to his plate and his fork would start working. Sorting, arranging. You couldn't call it eating. But not this boy; he could eat.

Meg had come to see the dinner table as a compass. First a vanishing at the foot, at the father's spot, the south. Then at Katie's seat: poof, no west. The needle of family flickered only to Charlie in the east, the tried-and-true east, and Meg at north.

Tonight, shamed by this boy's earnest, unadulterated eating, Meg had forced herself to talk over dinner, to single-handedly talk all directions back on the map. Once she got going, the answerable questions came in a deluge.

How was school today? Oh, she already asked him that? Yes, tell me again, then.

Did it feel cold to him? It *was* cold, wasn't it? She would go check the thermostat. Fifty-five, she called. How did that happen? The automatic timer clicks to night-low only after eleven. Surely it wasn't after eleven.

Did he like the stew, or did he find it, as she did, gummy?

Good, he answered emphatically. And filling. So filling that he didn't feel like cookies. Another clue. Charlie always perked up at the mention of cookies, although Meg had suspected the enthusiasm was feigned, to make him seem like a normal kid.

If she didn't mind, he said, he would just go to bed.

She noticed the clock. Midnight? How did that happen? Yes, you better go to bed. She spoke firmly, mustering discipline, as though he had not already been clearing his plate to head upstairs.

After that, she heard constant faint tapping overhead, him trying not to make a sound as he moved around the wide pine planks of Charlie's floor.

The car stopped running.

She went to the window. It must have rained and frozen. Everything was glazed. Trees, telephone wires, the rutted dirt road. A hall of mirrors outside. Jeff crossed the yard to the front path, the visitor's entrance, rather than coming in the mudroom door.

Finally he arrived, stamping his boots on the stoop for a good long time. Meg hurried to the couch, to reclaim the moral high ground that mounts when you wait sitting down. You lose it when you stand, when you cross the room, when you brush the curtain open to watch the once-and-future man of the house move through the crust of night.

The door opened slowly, a resistant creak. Jeff, looking exactly like Jeff. So his face was brighter with wind and night and rain, his clothes darker. Jeff in bad weather was all.

He came halfway inside and fanned the door in front of him; it played like an instrument. "Winter," he said, fingering the hinges. "You have to oil these. There's WD-40 in the—"

"Jeff."

"Okay, okay," he said.

"Are you wet?" *Are you icy?* she might have asked playfully, if he had been coming home after a short trip. But he had been on the road for most of the last year. He *arrived* home more than he *was* home.

"I made good time. I left Toronto about six-thirty." He looked to the pulse side of his wrist. "No watch? Boy, I really left in a hurry. And I left with a dead cell phone. I figured instead of stopping to call from the interstate, I'd just *get* here."

"And here you are." She couldn't help this wedge of anger.

"What time is it, anyway?"

"Four-thirty. Strange time to have someone arrive." She brushed her voice with conciliation and tried to sit perfectly still. Any action released into the room would send Jeff back out the door.

He counted on fingers. "Ten hours? It's an eleven-hour trip," he said, *amazed*.

"So, no traffic?"

"Rush hour at the Canadian border, you mean? Or the midnight shift letting out in Rochester?"

He laughed a little, tried anyway. The awkward laughter was fluffed up by a sudden gust of wind.

"Why don't you shut the door? Sit down, stay awhile."

An obedient wind sucked the door shut.

Jeff settled in to the inside of the house: the father called home from a business trip. "Okay. What's the matter?" he asked. "Why didn't he want to get off the bus?"

She blurted a quick I-give-up laugh. For all Jeff knew, Charlie'd hurt his knee at recess. She envied Jeff his question, the question Ben must have presented him over the phone, the question whose answer could be something like, Poor little guy was afraid we were having seitan for dinner again. Or, he had an asthma attack or a stomachache. Or, was punishing me so I'd get him a puppy. Wanted attention. Wanted his father to come home.

"Oh, Jeff. It's such a long story."

"Got a long time," he said. He took off his coat, squared it in front of him, and slapped it on the back like a tennis partner. "It's four-thirty in the morning. Where am I going to go?"

He looked around, as if there used to be a place to hang a coat in the living room, then he settled it over his arm.

"First," she said, "sorry to make you drive through the night."

"Don't do that." He shook his head. "I mean, don't worry about that."

He started in on his pacing. He was a pacer. Occupational habit, pacing off a site as a way to get a quick measure. The layman would be surprised how accurate it was, he'd said. A good architect could get his precision down to that of a standard yardstick.

"I know your project's heading to construction and it's a bad time to come home."

"No, no," he said. "Why don't you just tell me what happened. What was wrong. How everyone is doing now."

"*Now?* Everyone's fine now. The problem is not *now*, Jeff-to-the-rescue."

"*Then*, then." He stopped, held up his hands in surrender. "Last week. I don't know. I really don't. But I *want* to know. Trust me, I didn't just drive ten hours to fight with you. Tell me the whole story. Let's take it from the top."

Pacing again, he looked like he was trying to dodge the very whole story he'd just asked for.

"You're in the house," he started, "or whatever, and the bus stops in front. Last stop, long trip." His voice ebbed and flowed as he headed toward and away, toward and away. "Then what? He's just sitting inside the bus? Is he mad? Is he hurt? Did something happen at school? Or with you?"

"Okay." Meg took a deep breath. "When the bus stopped at the house, no one got out for the longest time. Then Sandy did. Only Sandy."

Jeff sat down, laying his jacket like a dog at his feet.

"You know it's going to be a long afternoon," she said, "when the driver gets off the bus before the kid."

"What did Sandy say? Had he told Sandy anything was wrong? Where were you?"

"He didn't say anything," she said. "Neither of them did. I was waiting at the front door. Not waiting, exactly. I kept *coming* to the door, over and over, thinking I'd just poke my head out in time to see him hop into the mudroom."

Jeff moved to the edge of the seat, then actually sat on his hands, to prevent himself, she knew, from spooling them *come on come on*. "Okay," he said. "So you're at the door . . ."

"I kept poking my head out. The whole thing was taking so long. It's usually a nothing thing, getting off that bus, a millisecond that you don't even notice. Just two times of day coming together, like a line in painting is nothing more than two edges coming together. Charlie at school, Charlie at home. It wasn't supposed to be a whole time of day in itself."

She was drawn to this part of the story as she had been drawn to the threshold of the doorway, again and again, when no one got off the bus, and, still, no one got off the bus.

"So, you went outside, got on the bus yourself?" Here was Jeff trying to be patient, sitting on his hands, jacket heaped and ready to go an arm's length away.

"Yes. After I don't even know how long, I went outside and got on the bus."

"And?"

Thinking of it now, she realized she had been sick to her stomach when she first saw the boy, such discordant sensory information wreaking havoc on her system.

"Was he not feeling well?" Jeff said. "Was it an asthma attack?"

"No, he was fine. Perfectly fine."

"Was he angry? Were *you* angry? Did he do something wrong?"

"Perfectly well behaved." That argyle sweater loomed in her mind. Where had that thing come from?

"And he's upstairs now and everything's fine?"

All Jeff wanted was the word *fine*, so he could get in the car and return to work.

"It's not him, Jeff," she said. "I know it sounds crazy. This is the first time I've said it out loud. It's just not Charlie."

"What?"

"I went onto the bus, saw this boy sitting there who I thought was Charlie. Of course I did. He's the only one left, the bus is right in front of our house. And he looks just like—*almost* like—him. So you'd think, right?"

"Yes, I'd think . . ."

"But it's not." She lowered her voice. "It's not Charlie."

"What did he say?"

"'Hi,'" she said, chirping.

Jeff smiled, and she did. Outside, ice cracked.

"No, really," she said. "He said hello, nice as can be. I asked about school, and, you'll be happy to know, it was fine today. Tuna melt for hot lunch. Never mind the salt, he likes salt."

Jeff was trying to blink sense into this, opening and closing his eyes, deliberate and periodic as Morse code. "What did Ben say? Or Sandy?"

It occurred to her that the sheriff must have called Jeff from this house while she sat on the bus with the boy. Sandy might have come inside, as well. The house seemed on the other side of familiar, turned inside-out like a sock, a place where outsiders conducted business while those who lived here were trapped outside.

"Ben, Sandy, too, seemed extraordinarily concerned about the bus. Gotta get the bus off the road, gotta stick to the designated route hours. Like that. As for the boy—"

"*The boy?*"

"The two of us, let's just say. As for the two of us, that was up to me. As usual."

"Meg. I'm here. I'm home. What do you want from

me?" She must have stiffened. "Wait, wait. I don't mean it like that, however you heard it. What I mean is, What would you like me to do? Should I talk to him? Is he upstairs? Let me go upstairs and see for myself."

But he didn't go anywhere. He stood and blinked, stood and blinked. He was at a loss for how to be at a loss.

"Right?" he said. "Isn't that what I should do?"

"You're the father," she said. "Shouldn't you know?"

He climbed the stairs so slowly she thought he might never make it. This was Jeff—always *on his way*. "I'm on my way," he would say from the road, on the cell. "I'm on my way," he would call from the barn or the basement. "I'm on my way," he must have said to Ben Handke.

Footsteps, finally overhead, slowed even more as he approached Charlie's room, each step smaller than the one before, as hers had been down the bus corridor.

She hadn't been upstairs yet herself. When they came in from the bus, she walked straight through the house and left again through the mudroom door. She had gotten as far as starting the car when she noticed him standing in the side doorway, his hand cocked.

Whether he was waving good-bye or motioning her to stop she wasn't sure, but he did get across one message: she couldn't very well get in the car and drive around frantically. This boy might need something from her. He might need to know where the bathroom was or what room he should stay in. He might be hungry and need dinner.

So she'd gone back inside, to the front hallway, as unsure where to go and what to do as he was. The two of them milled around until she said, "Why don't you go upstairs and change before dinner?" *Get out of that godawful argyle sweater that does not look like a child's.*

He'd nodded and started to the stairs.

The car keys, bunched with several others, jangled on their own in her hand. He turned around nervously.

"For the somethingth time," she'd said, "I'm not going anywhere."

She'd shooed him upstairs again, and he'd gone reluctantly.

She had tossed the keys to the empty plant stand by the door, and they landed with a clatter. A brief scrambling of footsteps overhead, but he had not reappeared.

Now she pictured Jeff sitting at the edge of the bed, as he did with the wounded or the weak, his hands craving a pliers, a two-by-four, a drafting pencil, something he knew what to do with.

Charlie had known sooner than anyone that Jeff would eventually leave. Meg had watched him put himself in his father's path—literally. He would stand in the side doorway when he heard Jeff's car. When Jeff was working in the basement woodshop or out in the barn, Charlie would sit at the head of the stairs or lie on the slate walkway, just in case his mother called his father upstairs or inside.

Maybe she could use Jeff as bait, plant him out in the barn or in his car in the driveway. See if Charlie, desperate to see his father, comes running home. Powdery, slight boy with hair tending to fluff rather than kink, round eyes made rounder by the smallness of his face. Pale almost to the point of translucence and breathing rapidly, unlike this new fresh-faced and freckled boy. Sometimes his mother could swear that the friction of his labored breath was all that kept Charlie weighted to earth.

A weight bore down on *her*, the weight of Charlie's not knowing Jeff was home. Who knew how long Jeff would stay? Charlie would hate himself (he was given to that) if he missed his father, missed his father because he himself was missing, when that was the very reason Jeff was here at all. Charlie had a habit of outfoxing himself—victor turned vanquished before the sixty-pound thing knew what had happened.

She picked up the portable phone next to her. "Charlie," she said in a regular speaking voice. "Your father's here." She had not depressed the TALK button; her words fell flat and dead against the closed-off phone. She dropped the handset, a hot potato. It crashed to the floor.

"What's that?" Jeff called from upstairs.

"I dropped the phone."

He hurried to the rescue.

The back panel had come off. Something to fix!

"Well?" she said.

But he was concentrating single-mindedly on his repair job, as if he had to connect intricate coaxial cables and fiber-optic lines rather than simply snap a piece of plastic in place.

"Well?" she prompted.

"If *you* don't know . . ." He drifted off, phone in hand using all his focus.

"A little help, please." Pursed lips, she sounded like herself when the kids were younger and the union between the parents was distilled down to tight pleas for help.

"Boy, Meg," Jeff said, not looking up. "What am I supposed to say? It sure looks enough like him."

"Enough?"

Imagine, she thought, children as approximations. Then again, in a sense they were. Each time your child returned home, he was an approximation of who you had sent out into the world that morning. And each morning, he was an approximation of who you'd tried to seal with a kiss the night before.

"Listen," Jeff went on, "he's asleep in Charlie's room, lying in Charlie's bed, wearing Charlie's pajamas."

She tried to picture the boy as Jeff did, as Charlie: asleep in his too big room, where he had huddled all the furniture together in the near corner and gotten Meg's permission to draw a giant X over the far floor in chalk so the furnace would know not to go there because the oversized house was hard to heat; lying in the junior bed that was too small for him, but Jeff had built it—"simple platform," Jeff'd said, "no big deal"—so he refused to graduate to a full-size bed, even though his father had promised to make that one, too; in candy-cane pajamas (Christmas gift), so twisted up half the time that it dizzied her when she checked on him in the middle of the night and tried to right him in all that diagonal striping.

"Which ones?" she said.

"Which pajamas? I don't remember. I don't know, the sheets and blankets were all bunched up, and . . . Jesus, Meg, if you want to test me after I drove all night and gave up who knows how many days on the job—

"Damn it!" he interrupted himself. He had inadvertently snapped the phone together. Job over. He stared at it for a moment, then looked up.

"Isn't there something we can *check*, papers or something?" he said.

"His driver's license?" she said. "His passport?"

His breathing. They could check his breathing. That way, they—*she*—could tell at least if they had another asthmatic on their hands. But she feared that such an intimate act, listening to breathing, was something she could get in trouble for later, when this child was returned to his rightful owner and was forced to report all that had happened to him in the Landry-Carroll house.

They could check his elbows, his knees. Charlie had clicky joints, a no-harm, no-foul condition of Jeff's that was something short of double-jointed. That was about the only thing Charlie had inherited from Jeff. Mostly, he looked like Meg, the fair skin and red hair, eyes so thin a brown that they appeared the same color as the hair. Both parents were tall. Meg was solid, big-boned, and Jeff lanky. Charlie was slight, but it was hard to tell which way he would go; he had not yet, as Dr. Ireland put it, "entered the growth sweepstakes." Katie, five years older and a girl, certainly had. At thirteen, her limbs were growing like they were trying to get away. Her dark hair was as moppy as Jeff's, her thick eyebrows and green eyes his thick eyebrows and green eyes. The mother, the switching yard, had steered Jeff to Katie, herself to Charlie. He had not yet started to get the freckles that redheaded children get in summer but his skin was that kind of pale, blank slate ready for the sun to smudge a little life into. He had a whorly cowlick in back, square fingers, and toes that defied the usual descending order. She wondered if Jeff could describe Charlie's fingers and toes.

"The hair looks different," Meg said. "That's one thing. The hair's all wooly."

"That's new?" Jeff rubbed his face long and hard. "I'm sorry. I can't seem to tell anything. I've been away. For all I know, he is our son. He looks a little older than he did three months ago, but—"

"Try two days ago. Not three months ago."

"I'm sorry," he said. "That's all I know, three months ago. It might be him and it might not, for all I can tell from the back of a head at five A.M. Kids change. Or they don't change. But what do I know? If you don't know, for Christsakes, if *you* can't say, how can I?"

If she had sent Charlie up to Toronto to visit his father and *this* boy had gotten off the bus, Jeff would have said, "How was your trip? Did you hit any traffic?" Only secretly, maybe not even admitting it to himself, would he have thought: I barely recognize my own son.

The first of January, Jeff took an open-ended project in Toronto, and the previous year he had been on the road as much as possible. He'd been taking projects farther and farther away and requiring more and more on-site presence. He and Meg talked very little about his new schedule, as they had been talking very little about anything. Common ground diverged by the year, by the day, by the hour. Perhaps the Toronto project had looked especially tempting to Jeff from the vantage point of the TV room, where he had been sleeping on the pull-out couch whenever he was home.

"Did he tell you about that goose we've been watching? 'We have to call it something,'" she imitated, deepening her voice rather than raising it as she would have with her still thin-voiced son. It was the boy on the bus whose register she was after.

"No, he was sleeping."

"Really sleeping? Not faking?"

"Lying there like a lump. Does he do that, pretend to be sleeping?"

Used to be, Charlie would pretend badly, by holding his breath until a cough or a gulp popped blowfish cheeks. Or he'd whisper, "I'm sleeping pretty well. See?" to make sure she was really there, really seeing him. But lately, she could no longer say.

And *this* boy? She could imagine him feigning sleep, knowing that a good boy should be asleep at five in the morning. She could imagine him succumbing to the temptation to see life without yourself, present but not accounted for, fly on the wall, observer at your own funeral.

"Strange that we have any geese at all right now," Jeff said, looking out the window. "Too early for them to be coming north. Much too late for heading south."

He snapped his fingers onto other things. "Fingerprints, dental records. Hard evidence. Let's get some answers here."

She had been thinking of answers as a flower or fruit out of season. Dormant, gone for now. But Jeff was ever the architect: *so many feet long by so many feet wide by so many feet deep*.

"Plenty of people keep records of a child," he continued. "Teachers, the pediatrician, even the sheriff could tell—"

"Teachers? Doctors?" she said. "We could call in the truant officer, the dog catcher, the zoning commissioner. But we're the *parents*. Shouldn't it be up to us to know?"

"There's so much you can do with technology these days. Fingerprints. Blood. DNA, if we wanted. From a pillowcase or a hairbrush."

"He's not a criminal. He's just a boy," she said. "Whoever he is."

"All right," Jeff said. "Let's sketch this thing out." He riffled through newspapers and magazines on the coffee table. He unnested three side tables until he found pen and paper. First step in the search for answers.

He cleared a space on the coffee table, spread a cocktail napkin, and poised pen to paper. "Let's write down what we know and what we don't. Make a list."

Before he wrote a word, he unfolded more napkins, building himself a bigger canvas. He laid another row, and another, until the whole coffee table was covered in napkins.

Yes, Jeff? Meg readied for answers. *Go on.*

He was doodling, it turned out, a quick, sure sketch of their son. From Jeff's controlled hand, another approximation: Charlie in fibrous lines. Remarkable verisimilitude on the leeching tissue, and not bad for an architect. Meg found herself thinking something she hadn't thought in years: Jeff can do anything. She, the supposed artist of the two, would have done no better—not now, certainly.

He stopped. He held the pen still. It bled into the napkin like a bullet wound. He crumpled it up and put his head in his hands.

Meg shook his shoulder lightly. To rouse him, to get him back. "What were you trying to do?"

"I have no idea," he said. His face was red and his hands were inky. A few lines had printed faintly on his forehead. He was a map.

"You were going to write down what we know and what we don't know," she prompted.

"No idea."

"Too bad," she said. "I was with you for a minute there."

3

DAWN DOES STRANGE THINGS to a fully lit house, absorbs light from the rooms and spreads it across the yard. Once inside and outside had equilibrated, Meg and Jeff could stay put no longer. They had been hovering near the front door like children waiting for rain to pass.

Not until they were safely down the road did she look over her shoulder at the house. The front door appeared closed. Mercifully, Charlie's bedroom window was a dark square, a one-way mirror. She did not want to see a boy outlined there, making a wish that she was still downstairs even though he could perfectly well see two adults cross the yard and head down the road. Did he know—could he tell by its bright-red urgency—that there was a PANIC button next to Charlie's bed, one that connected, through its QuicKonnect operator, to 911 and the on-call pediatrician?

She felt both an urgency and a waywardness, a need to sprint on the one hand, but, on the other, where to go? The road, bordered by sloping woods, seemed as precarious as a balance beam.

"Remember 'the march of April'?" she said, mustering a little nostalgia.

Underfoot, the road felt plump. Runoff churned through the bunched woods. Tributaries drew everywhere like so many pulled threads. Jeff used to call mud season the march of April when they first moved here and the seasons were noteworthy.

He nodded, digging a boot in the mud. "Pretty soggy," he said. "Get a lot of snow this winter?"

"It was a bad winter."

"It was a bad winter in Toronto, too," he said. "If that's any consolation."

"Good."

"Cold *and* snow. Usually it's one or the other. I don't know how it was both this year. Perception, maybe. Just felt like we were getting it from both sides. No, I think it was more than that. We broke a record, I heard, for number of below-zero days in one month, fifteen in January. Then February was record snowfall."

She stuck out her hand, feigning introduction. "Meg Landry. Nice to meet you," she said. "Jeff, we're talking about the *weather*."

"Okay." Jeff held up his hands, a sign of both surrender and stop-it. "Let's not go down this road."

Meg looked at her feet, considering the actual road they were going down, and was brought up short—by the suddenness of being in each other's company again, by the randomness of making a home in this patch of the world, by the inability to put the right words to anything.

She had spent a lot of time on these roads. Since Charlie was a baby. She would drop Katie off somewhere—even then, as a five-year-old, Katie was always abroad: at kindergarten, at a friend's house, dance class, gymnastics, Little Artists Workshop—and Meg would drive and drive. Often, she drove all the way to Canada, answering "business" to the "business or pleasure?" question at the border. "A gallery show," she would invent, or "master classes." Once she told the guard she was taking her son for experimental medical treatment. The sound of it, and the gravity of the border official's expression, haunted her into never doing that again. She didn't return to Canada for quite a while afterward—and didn't return again once Jeff started taking work there. She drove instead the high, empty roads to New Hampshire or the better-traveled routes to upstate New York.

From the beginning, Jeff put up a good fight to be the one who leaves, spending more and more time in the office, building a practice, supporting a family. *Please.* Even when he was home he was hard to find, working in the barn or the basement, reinsulating the attic, laying stones to get better flow in the stream that bordered the property.

Along back roads, Meg would pretend, as you can in the country, that reality was not hard and fast. The presence of a baby in the car seat, however, eventually snapped her back to her life—a mother whose plans for herself were temporarily on hold. She would jab at a canvas whenever the kids were asleep or away, but it always seemed minutes at a time. She would squeeze paint on a palette, commit the brush, and barely invest the canvas with color when something would call her away. Just *make* yourself go back to it every day, Jeff would say. Grit your teeth and pick up right where you left off. Or else he'd say, Don't worry about it. It's not putting food on the table. *Please*, I don't mean it like that. You're doing it because you want to, and, for Christsakes, if you don't want to . . .

They'd come to Vermont in the first place so they could manage on Jeff's income alone and she could paint. And raise the kids free from the commerce and competition that had marked her own childhood—concerts, recitals, lessons, master teachers, not for her but for her sister, Holly, the piano prodigy in an overeducated family that owned a growing chain of music stores in urban and suburban Boston. Both girls had started taking piano lessons at the same time, Meg six, Holly four, from a student of their mother's, until they were good enough or old enough to withstand being taught by their mother. Then, once Holly broke away with prodigious talent, she got a piano *coach* and Meg slowly won her freedom by refusing to practice. Meantime, she discovered that she liked and was good at painting and drawing, a double-edged rebellion that had nothing to do with either music or practicality.

The yearlong death of Meg's father—"the last of the great smokers," he'd call himself, playing with a pipe cleaner or a reamer even after he was forbidden to smoke—finally precipitated the move, Vermont looming as a respite from a mother who had given herself over to depression well before her husband's actual death and from a sister who called from the road whenever she could. To help, she'd say, not helping at all. That house, Meg still remembered, was a minefield of static blare and silence. Her mother had taken to the guest bedroom, where she kept the lights off and the shades drawn. Her father, meanwhile, had created an electric force field in his sickroom. Television, radio, overhead and tabletop light, an oscillating fan, an old miniature player piano—any combination of droning and humming and whirring to ward off death.

Jeff liked the idea of a country architecture practice and had apparently always wanted to own a barn. They had not married, Meg and Jeff, in order to further their vision of a reflective life unencumbered by tradition, with budding children who would determine their own paths rather than have them be determined by—or against—the parents.

She almost bumped into Jeff. He had stopped to watch two deer foraging at the edge of the woods.

"I heard on the news that our deer population has really gotten out of hand," he said, "that it's driving everyone crazy. Farmers, gardeners, the state highway patrol."

The animals turned, gazed at them in that frankly doe-eyed way, but didn't move. From an art class on the eye, The Eye of the Beholder, Meg knew a thing or two about how each couple saw the other. Deer, with their eyes all rods and no cones, were color-blind, saw her red hair as muddy as the road, if they could make it out at all. They saw Meg and Jeff as crude approximations of human forms but could judge them well enough that way—as friend or foe—day, night, or this, twilight. Deer made the most of dawn's ultraviolet light with their *tapetum lucidum* ("bright carpet"), a reflective membrane that reemits light to the retina a second time and, at a certain angle, makes the nocturnal eye appear to glow in the dark.

"There've been more catamount sightings, too," Jeff continued, "and it's not even full-blown spring. They're coming out of the mountains, apparently, for the smaller deer."

He looked around. "Have we gone past it?"

"What?" she said.

"The dingle. You said we should go to the dingle."

"*I* did?" The oddness of witnessing daybreak made it hard to keep track of things.

"Back at the house. Not ten minutes ago. You said we should go check down at the dingle, where we used to look for Bear." He used an old nickname of Katie's, one that she hated and now forbade her mother to use. "Though I don't know what good it will do."

Nor did she. But she had indeed suggested it. Now she remembered. She had needed to leave the house, if just to walk, get some air. She knew Jeff would need a destination. And a reason. "Maybe we'll find something, some clue down there," she had said. "Something of Charlie's."

In truth, Charlie never went down to the dingle, the streamside flat at the bottom of a ravine about a half mile from the house, where all the other neighborhood kids hung out, where Meg knew to look for Katie whenever she had been told to come home. Her mother needed her help, her mother needed her *right here, please,* where she could see her. *On time, please,* I have enough to worry about with him. You're just jealous, Katie would say. You're just jealous because you can't play outside and I can. Which Meg would punish her for, or, increasingly, just let go, exhausted by her daughter and her son in such different ways.

Meg let Jeff walk ahead, purposeful even though he didn't seem to have faith in the purpose. She lagged further and further, as if a different pace might lead to a different place. *Distance equals rate times time.* Everything, it turns out, can be rendered as a variable.

Her rods and cones filled with the woods, trees in all directions, as far as the eye's parts could see. Charlie was about the same girth as a small birch—an infinite number of which she could see in any one frame of vision on this half-mile walk along this single road in this one tiny town in the least populous state in the country.

"Children very rarely just disappear," she still remembered Ben Handke saying years ago, the one time she panicked over Katie and called the Sheriff's Department when she didn't come home and couldn't be found at the dingle.

Looking around, Meg could see Ben was wrong. Anyone, anything could disappear right here, on this half-mile walk along this single road in this one tiny town . . .

"This it?" Jeff called to her when he got to an opening in the trees. "Hello?" he hollered into the woods, hands cupped around his mouth like a child playing explorer.

Meg listened for anger, as Charlie would have done.

Charlie was always courting his father's elusive anger. The few times he did something wrong, he would wait for his father to come home, then wait further for him to get mad. He would brush up against Jeff, as though passion were pollen and could be released that way. With Meg or Katie, Jeff would tighten his jaw, hyperextend his fingers, and issue a razor-thin order or insult between clenched teeth when he was mad. But he would keep even this pinched anger from Charlie.

Poor Charlie never seemed to get bad behavior right. It never touched anyone but him. Katie could raise her parents' blood pressure plenty: refusing to come when called (and called and called and called—and then outright *searched for*); disobeying orders right and left with a "What are you going to do to me?" But before he got anywhere even halfway defiant, Charlie would hyperventilate, then cough and wheeze, sometimes making himself sick to his stomach, which, of course, would let the air out of any parent's anger. Or he'd break something of his own, a toy or a game, which meant only that he could no longer play with that toy or game. Katie, meanwhile, destroyed things that weren't hers.

"Here?" Jeff stood at what was clearly a trail opening, much more of an entrance than Meg had remembered. She remembered having to brush aside so many branches from so many different sources that when she passed through and let them go, the woods seemed to snap closed behind her.

But this was it. You could hear the stream below, a muffled rushing from this distance. The stream eventually ran to their yard. It could carry things back to the house. Floating sacrifices, Meg thought.

"Yes," she said. "I guess it is."

As soon as Jeff disappeared down the narrow path, the crowding of limbs and branches returned. Meg used a jacketed forearm, one of the body's more resilient parts, to scythe her way through the trees. Light was tentative anyway at this time of day. But in the woods, forget it. No color vision, no depth perception. Was this arm indeed attached to her? But wasn't it too far away? And now, hand in front of face, what color was flesh, anyway? Shouldn't there be some pink to this colorless gray?

Charlie would never have gone into these woods, where, *listen*, everything darts and brushes and haunts. Not to mention Jeff's catamounts and emboldened deer. Charlie would never have spent the night anywhere but his bedroom, in reach of the nebulizer, his mother, a pitcher of water, the PANIC button, which they called the PICNIC button, based on an earlier mispronunciation. Asthma was worse at night. The lungs tend to collect fluid when the body is lying down, Dr. Ireland explained. Like a saucer in a rainstorm, he'd said. Not a cup or a bowl, he added by way of assurance—not enough to drown in, but enough to make life difficult for the little guy. Dr. Ireland's words.

This access path, steep and switchbacked, required a child's center of gravity. She had to let herself go, trusting— as you trust an airplane to fly—that she would get where she was going before the slope, or she, gave way entirely. Her vertigo resurfaced, with the split sense of at once heading toward a destination and losing ground, with the body-falling-out-from-beneath-itself sensation of a falling dream.

Then again, if Charlie had truly wanted to disappear, the dingle would be an excellent choice. No one would ever think to look there because it was a neighborhood frontier and everyone knew he was no frontiersman.

"Hello . . ." Jeff again, calling ahead.

No one would think to look there except his father, who didn't really know him at all.

Flat land. She looked up the steep downhill she'd traversed, but she could no longer remember being anywhere but this flat ground. Next to Jeff. From now on, she would be a good mother, no matter the boy. She would love him *as if* he were Charlie until all doubt withered and disappeared, as husks of dead insects do even from corners no one can reach. Just disappear over time, swapping themselves molecule by molecule back to earth and air. Dust to dust.

She kept her eye on the back of Jeff's head—such thick, beautiful hair—amid snapping-shut branches, as they walked the short jag of a path to the streamside clearing that was the dingle.

"This is where they play?" he said. "Not much here."

And there wasn't! It was a clearing, with all the relief a clearing offers. The patch of silvery wet-looking silt was as open and straightforward as a parking space. The expanse of flat rock that bordered it suggested picnic. Or nap.

This was where the neighborhood children passed entire afternoons, not surfacing until called and called and called for dinner. This was where Katie threatened to live out the rest of her days because her brother got everything he ever wanted because of his stupid asthma. Lately, this was where Meg, too, had taken to passing an afternoon now and then because, in truth, he got *nothing* he ever wanted because of his stupid asthma—something a mother had to get away from every once in a while.

Jeff stepped carefully onto the rocks, avoiding the streamside silt as if it were sacred ground of another people. Or a crime scene. There were indeed footprints. A child's? An adult's? Hard to tell, they were so faint. Who knew how long prints lasted on such fluid earth? Perhaps they were days old, perhaps only hours.

She wanted to tromp the footprints into oblivion. Into her own. Then at least they'd know whose footprints these were. But she'd started to think of the silt as quicksand, and she followed Jeff up onto the rocks.

A beam of honest-to-God daylight filtered through the trees, studding the silt with diamonds and gold. Meg wondered if Jeff finally saw it: how the place could capture a hair-trigger imagination. The sudden sun illuminated all the possibilities of what they might find down here.

Who's the sun god? Apollo? Jeff would know, but this she couldn't ask. So she made a pact with the sun itself. If there's no Charlie here, lying in the woods, small and prone, wet and matted . . . if there's no body here, then give her that boy back, the boy from the bus, polite and redheaded and knowing a thing or two about the Landry-Carroll family, and that would be good enough. Jeff could be right. Enough could be good enough.

"Hellooooo." Jeff's hollers were beginning to sound like a joke, since he and she were clearly the only two around. To a child, it might have sounded like a game the adults were playing with each other.

"Do you really think he'd hide down here?" Jeff asked.

Hide? The innocence of the word hiked up the prone body she'd been picturing, yanked it upright into a live little boy. The word transformed something grave and horrible— a search whose end was known, in the pit of the stomach, from the beginning—into an extravagant, indoor-outdoor game of hide-and-seek.

But she knew Charlie would not be hiding. He hated to, ever since a game of hide-and-seek three or four years ago ended in Katie's running for a parent, someone to open the wheezing steamer trunk in the basement. There he was, puffy- and red-faced, captive in enemy territory: wool blankets. After that, he would hide only in the open, or announce himself loudly. "I'm going behind the couch." Katie would torture him by *not* looking. Couldn't care less.

It occurred to Meg only now: maybe Katie was scared of what she'd find.

A jagged vein stood out in Jeff's temple. Meg imagined the crooked thing stopping blood flow like a kinked hose. She squatted on the rock and pressed a finger, just a finger, into the ground below. As soon as she took it away, the silt blurred the hole, fading it as if with time. Those faint footprints could be from seconds ago.

She could tell from the state of Jeff's brow that he had a million questions for her, something she had not seen in

years. They had met in art school—Jeff studying architecture, Meg fine arts—and in the beginning their common
ground was rich and apparent. They used to pepper each
other with questions.

"Do you?" he said, surveying the area like a seaman,
hand visoring his eyes. "Do you really think he's down here
hiding?"

However little she knew, Jeff knew less.

"No," she said, "I never did."

Here was a chance to see his father. Charlie never would
have hidden through that. Even if he had played out the
scene one step further, wanting his mother to be alone with
his father for a minute, his excitable lungs would have
kicked in. He would have coughed, given himself away.
Charlie's asthma was more easily manifest when he was
nervous or excited. "Emotional histamines," Dr. Ireland
called it, although once he was coughing, he *was* coughing.
His mother still had to rub his back, still had to clamp her
hands over his chest like a second rib cage (the first, his own,
felt like it could collapse in a stiff wind). And the doctor still
had to manage a thoracic system inflamed from all that
coughing, a stomach weak from digestive interruption, an
immune system depressed from lack of sleep and nutrition.

Yes, it was possible that he was working young mind
over young body, but he worked it well enough to spend the
day coughing. The doctor himself had pointed out that
coughing was both symptom and cause; it signaled the onset
of an asthma attack at the same time that it worsened the
attack, further tightening the airways.

"If you don't think he's down here," Jeff said, "then why on earth are we?"

"Do you have any better ideas?" She fingered her own temples, seeking a crooked vein like Jeff's, somewhere to stop the blood.

"I feel like I'm going to explode." He rubbed his forehead. "But not with ideas."

Meg had given herself a headache at the temples. She had to sit down with her hands over her eyes. Darkness. This self-induced nocturne unleashed a misplaced wave of nightlike exhaustion. She couldn't remember when she'd last slept.

"There he is!" Jeff said.

She opened her eyes. Her vision approximated a star-spangled sky. She could not see the light of day. Gradually, the streamside came back into focus, branches and leaves quivering along the path.

"Charlie?" Meg whispered.

A glimpse of red hair, ducking behind a birch. Hiding, after all?

She hurried across slick rock.

He came out from behind the tree. Meg stopped short, caught her balance, and shielded her eyes against the gloating sun, which lit that woolly hair, bleached that argyle sweater under an unzipped windbreaker.

She drew back onto the rock, back to Jeff.

The boy stood in the quicksand silt, and the sun tucked into the woods, unable to exact its promise. She wouldn't touch him, couldn't get any closer. She put Jeff, of all people, between the two of them.

"Well?" Jeff said.

"*You* tell *me*," she said. "What if I left it up to you? What then?"

He reached down and cuffed the boy playfully on the chin.

The child flinched, apparently not knowing how good this father was at holding back anger.

"Hey, Chappy," Jeff said. "Fancy meeting you here."

The boy was squirming his arms out of his sweater and jacket. He packed himself strong across the torso while his empty sleeves hung in a separate state—apologetic, forlorn.

"What's he doing?" Jeff said to Meg. Then, to the boy, "What is it you're doing?"

"I'm a little cold."

"Put your clothes on properly," Meg said.

"Has he been here the whole time, or did he follow us?" Jeff to Meg.

The boy did as he was told. For the mother, he made motions of putting his jacket back on, squirming, jabbing an elbow toward a sleeve. For the father: "I followed you. I wondered where you were going."

Jeff stirred with an idea. "Listen," he said, tapping the rock under his feet, "do you know what this is called?"

"A rock?" the boy ventured.

"I mean this place," Jeff clarified. "Where we are right now. Do you know what this place is called?"

The boy shook his head.

"Think," Jeff said. He gestured once more around the premises—grandly and desperate for approval, like a real estate agent, or God showing Moses the land of Canaan.

Then, to Meg, "Maybe kids don't call it that anymore."

"Of course they do," she said. "They still call it the dingle." How long *had* he been gone?

"Oh, the dingle?" the boy said. "I knew *that*. I thought you meant it had a realer name, like from the dictionary."

"Do you know where this stream comes out?" Jeff asked.

Again, the boy shook his head.

"You have no idea?"

Nope, no idea.

"Enough, Jeff," Meg said. And to the boy, "Behind our house."

"That's the same stream as ours?" he said, fidgeting foot to foot on the silt. The ground seemed firm under him, not quicksand at all. "Is it really? The same stream?"

"The very same," Jeff said. "Now that we have all this topography squared away, how about everybody heading home?"

When they climbed up to the road, Jeff announced he would go get Katie, that everyone should be home for Easter weekend. Everyone, including Dad. He strode back to the house, taut with a plan.

The boy, who seemed to intuit that he and Meg were in it alone again, kept drifting to the side of the road, picking up and naming stones. Mica he got right. After that, it was all random: granite, limestone, samsonite.

"Samsonite?" she couldn't help but ask. "What's samsonite?"

"This," he said, proffering a round yellowish pebble.

"What makes it samsonite?"

"The color," he said matter-of-factly. "And the shape. Everything, really."

Next, leaves. Maple he identified correctly. Oak, he called a slim ash leaf. Then, again randomly: birch, dogwood, peanut.

"Peanut?" Meg said. "A leaf from a peanut tree?"

"No," he said. "A leaf in the shape of a peanut."

She unfocused her eyes, tried to see just the boy's outline, no features, no discrete items of clothing. A boy in the shape of her son. A boy as a deer might see him.

As a painter, she had been trained to see the big picture first, to block it out, then draw her eye down to the specific. The big picture had Jeff far ahead, trying to make sense of this nonsense, as he might say. He was a small, dark figure receding into the road's vanishing point. Next to her, a blurred, inquisitive boy, not diminishing whatsoever, since he held the same relation to the horizon as she did.

"I don't think peanuts grow on trees," he said. "I think they grow on vines."

She heard a car in the distance. Katie would be furious when she was first pulled from class. But it would be her *father*, come to pick up her and her alone. She would spend the ride home knocking between fury and idolatry.

Meg had not yet summoned worry for her daughter. There was, after all, a surefire way to recognize Katie: all Meg had to do was spin her around, let her leave, and she would know for certain if it was Katie. Katie from the back. Yes, *that* Meg would recognize.

"Money doesn't grow on trees," the boy said, amusing himself.

The car approached. Meg shunted him to the edge of the woods. "The roads are muddy and slippery," she said. "Very dangerous to be walking here."

The green Jeep held to the middle of the road. It was Vince Palazzo, off to work. Waves all around.

The next car would surely be Jeff's.

The boy presented her a bouquet of leaves. Better than what she would be presented next—Katie's noisy complaints and Jeff's silent ones.

"You don't have to pick up every single thing on the side of the road," she said.

"Sorry." He burrowed his chin into his sweater.

Jeff had been summoned home *by law enforcement*, and it was still her alone with this one.

He lowered his eyes, then raised them, bright with an idea. He pulled his sweater over his nose like a bandit and held out a finger-thumb gun.

She slapped it away. "Not even in play," she said. She was hot with anger, shame and righteousness—a brittle mix particular to disciplining someone else's child.

Chin in his sweater, he opened and closed his mouth, gobbling.

"Get your face out of there. You'll suffocate." Fake gun had exposed real panic.

He did as he was told. "I wonder if he's going to wait," he said, fingering his damp-dark collar wistfully, "or if he's going to go get Katie without us."

Did he know that this father was always on the verge of leaving, or was this a lucky, likely guess, knowing fathers?

She quickened her pace so he had to skip every few steps to keep up. If a visiting child hadn't been right there at her heel, healthy bounce in his step, she would have broken into a run.

4

MEG FELT AS IF they had been gone for hours, but the front hall clock said seven. The sun could not have risen much before six-thirty; they had been gone a half hour at most. This is how time will pass from now on, she thought.

"Is that your sweater?" she asked Jeff, indicating the argyle sweater the boy was wearing.

"I can't say I remember it."

"What kind of a thing is that for a child to be wearing?" Then, to the boy, she said, "Did you get that sweater from our room?"

He shook his head. He pulled down his sleeves in order to roll them up. "Do you really think it might be yours?" he asked Jeff.

"Maybe something you or my mother got me for some holiday," Jeff said to Meg.

"Why don't you go upstairs and change?" she said. "There's a whole closet full of things that would be better than that. A sweatshirt, a fleece pullover."

The boy headed upstairs.

Jeff headed to the mudroom. "I'm on my way."

"No, wait," Meg said, remembering, following him. "Next week's her spring break. I said she could go on that ski trip." It would be Katie's first vacation alone with friends and a teacher/chaperone from school, and she had waged quite a battle with her mother to get permission.

"She can go on a ski trip another time. It's Easter weekend. I'm home. Charlie's . . . Something's going on with her brother. With all of us."

"Don't you think we have enough on our hands without the wrath of Katie? And it will be wrath, you know, although she seems to keep it from you."

"If something's happening at home," he said, "she should be home. Simple as that."

"Simple as that? You didn't hear her, Jeff. How nasty she can be when she wants something. I'd swear she gets it from my sister, except who can remember the last time they saw their Aunt Holly."

The denouement of Katie's plea: "There's never anything to do at home unless you're *you* and all you want to do is take care of a sick kid all the time."

"Maybe she can talk to him or help or something. Find out what's going on," Jeff said.

"Have you *met* our kids? They're in two completely different worlds. Katie barely talks to Charlie. All she ever is when it comes to him is annoyed."

"Maybe she can help *us*, then."

"You really don't know her at all, Dr. Spock, do you?"

"I'm just saying," he said, "we have to start somewhere."

"Next time, let's not start in front of the kids. When you announce something like 'I'm going to pick her up now' in front of him, it makes me the villain if I disagree."

"Okay," Jeff said. "Between you and me, I'm going to pick her up now."

The storm door did not shut right behind him, bouncing down like a just-abandoned rubber ball. Air leaked in, pungent with changing season. Meg felt something inside her slip free, perhaps her soul knocking its way out. Why not, she thought. Why not? On the other side of the storm door, naked trees kicked up in a breeze, nodding to a new presence. Her chest felt bruised, tight.

As she watched Jeff back out of the driveway, she thought of a book from her childhood, one that used to haunt her. She couldn't remember the title, but it was about a mouse who slept later and later each day, growing away from his family as sleep cycles diverged. The family never saw him, and soon they were beset with a vague sense of mourning. Gloomily, they moved mouseholes, now that they thought they were one mouse down. She could not recall what happened next and was quite sure there was a happy ending, but the family's move terrified her. It suggested that if you lose touch on a front as simple as sleep, you can lose everything.

From the kitchen window, Meg watched Jeff drive away with his headlights on in full daylight, already adjusted to life in Canada, where by law they drive with headlights on in full daylight.

The book that Katie had feared most when she was little was *Madeleine*. It made her scared of stomach pain, believing that it lands a child in the hospital and renders her an orphan (although now, as a teenager, she'd eagerly accept the latter, even at the cost of the former). For Charlie, the book was *Snip, Snap, Snur.* What seemed to bother him most in this Scandinavian happy-brothers series was the name Snur, which, of course, Katie called him relentlessly once she saw how it upset him.

Seven-twenty on the front hall clock. The day was here. There were two usual kinds of mornings. Good and bad. Good amounted to her waking her son up for school, battling his symptoms, real or fake, and his protests, trying to get some protein into him—eggs, high-protein toast, high-protein cereal, high-protein breakfast bar. Sometimes she resorted to cut-up tofu squares and canola oil.

Always encourage him to go to school, the doctor had advised. Asthma is not contagious, and children are almost always better off at school. As detrimental as the physical condition is the stigma of being sick, of being different. If they stay home too much, asthmatic children grow uncomfortable at school. They can become timid, unsure of themselves, and grow fearful of being out in the world. So please, Dr. Ireland had beseeched, treat him like a regular child, send him to school every morning. The nurse at Union Valley Lower was perfectly capable of administering the limited dose of epinephrine she was authorized to keep in her office.

Bad mornings followed sleepless nights in which she stayed by the side of his bed until he—and sometimes she—fell asleep. Bad mornings found Charlie still in bed and her camped on his floor, although lately the tables had been turning. More and more, bad mornings found *her* still in bed and Charlie camped on the hypoallergenic throw rug in the master bedroom.

Already, this morning was different, her downstairs, him upstairs.

There was, however, the same expanse of day and house in front of her. The same sense, standing in the foyer, that she could see forever, from the cavernous living room to the TV room entrance, from the separate dining room through the archway to the kitchen. The only thing that gathered close was an early April chill, with the house making its transition from underheated in winter to unheated in spring.

Had Jeff really been home at all?

The coffee table in the living room was still papered with napkins. Evidence. She sat down on the couch and slid the mosaical napkins around like puzzle pieces. What had Jeff been trying to do? They felt like nothing under her hand. She could feel every nick and nuance of the tabletop. She put a napkin over her mouth. You could breathe right through it, breathe a hole into it.

She lay down. When had she last slept? The question turned into a labyrinth of dead-ends. Not last night . . . not the night before . . .

She tried to keep herself from drifting off, since she

anticipated being awakened by slamming doors and a "This better be good because I'm supposed to be going on a ski trip in two days." She wanted to keep her guard up for that.

But she was porous with exhaustion. Porous as coral. Sea and sand sweeping in, sweeping out, eroding, returning such a thing as coral to the ocean. Undertows, riptides, drifting tides. Drifting in and out. And under, into the swirl of sleep, until she hit the coming-clear image of a dream. It was Katie, holding some kind of scepter, standing over a sleeping mother. Meg saw, amorphously at first and then quite vividly, that Katie was a queen, armed with a crown and red-and-ermine robes. In real life, Jeff had briefly called her Queen Katie, both mocking and trying to flatter his way into her graces. But Meg put a stop to that. No nicknames that make the situation worse, please, she had said. Her own father used to call her sister Dame Holly, just the sense of entitlement she needed to keep up a traveling schedule no matter what.

Katie had long been restless and bored out in the country, in a big farmhouse and a small family, school and friends too far away, mother too close, brother too much of a baby, father too gone all the time. She turned gloomy when Charlie began getting sicker, bilious when Jeff began staying away longer and longer. *Ma-aa-aa-ad.* Meg had developed a system of swinging the word polysyllabic to warn a returning Jeff of the level of their daughter's rage. Charlie was always calmer, never went beyond a single-syllable alarm.

The first line of defense was to leave her alone, next to get her her own phone line, then to buy her a TV for her bedroom. When nothing worked, they decided to let her go away to school—partly as a favor (she's so glum, let's *let* her out of the house), partly as a punishment (she's so nasty, let's *get* her out of the house).

She was indeed happy and befriended at school, if overly concerned about being popular, choosing her company according to the most transparent middle-school-girl hierarchy. When she was home, having spent her good graces in public, she was bitter and brooding with her mother and obsequious with her father. Then he would head back to Canada, and there Meg would be, alone with a teenage approximation of a daughter she had sent out into the world so long ago.

Nothing's more deleterious to sleep than anticipation— in this case, of arrival, but usually of an asthma attack, a coughing bout, or a crying jag. She had grown prescient, or at least insomniacal, and usually found herself awake a moment before trouble. Now, with Katie and Jeff expected any minute, Meg's nap only skimmed the surface, pooling broad rather than deep, touching this and that aspect of her life, making it at once more clear and refractive.

Looking-glass sleep swiveled to Sandy, and had Meg longing for him as a Vermonter in early April longs for spring. And, as with spring, what she was falling for in Sandy was the obvious: he came by every day. The beginning and end of each day, there was Sandy. Bus driver by weekday morning and late afternoon, farmer the rest of the time. He had sheep and goats, milk and cheese and wool, and a variety of designer greens that had recently become a big seller. He had news of the day and a desire to be with her. She knew he would come into her kitchen if given the chance, would prop himself against the counter, talking and listening while she cooked bread or mulled cider, vegetable stew or seitan again.

When had she and Jeff last lingered in the kitchen, over a cup of coffee at the beginning of the day or, at the end, a glass of wine or a brandy? No longer part of her habitual day, he proved difficult to locate in the borderland of an early-morning nap.

The smells that wafted from the kitchen were not of melting butter and eggs but of accusation. She *should* be cooking breakfast. She felt this obligation as clearly as she felt her heavy bones unable to move. She should be getting Charlie up for school, coaxing him into the day, talking him out of this or that excuse. Rise and shine. She should be making him the big breakfast that it smelled like the house itself was cooking to torment her, the big breakfast that he would never eat but at least he'd have a lot to contend with, a lot to push around.

Webbed in sleep, she shuffled into the kitchen with a vague sense of meeting her failure.

Instead, the kitchen bloomed with life, with cooking. The boy stood at the stove, crisping butter and eggs over a high heat. A mound of six or eight eggshells was heaped on the counter.

"Whoa," she said. "Can't cook so much over that high a heat."

He turned down the flame, which promptly flickered out.

Why hadn't Chappy thought of this? she wondered, mesmerized by the swirl of marbleized eggs. Why hadn't Charlie thought to cook for *her*, overcooking like this so no one kept track of whether a person got enough protein or appreciated a mother's cooking sufficiently.

"These burners are tricky," she said. "They take some getting used to. Let me do this."

He stood his ground, stirring the now-silent eggs, half raw, half burnt.

"Really," she said sternly. "I'm the mother. I'll do it."

He stepped away from the stove like a child reluctantly leaving television or a video game.

"But thank you," she said. "I should have said that first off."

He looked around the kitchen, sizing up its emptiness.

In the hanging three-tiered mesh basket, onions were sprouting shoots, potatoes were taking root midair. The other day—just *yesterday*—she had used onions and potatoes for stew. How had these hearty root vegetables declined so precipitously? Was time now flowing in all directions, over-running, a river spilling its banks to fill an empty house?

"Why don't you put some silverware around the dining room table," she said. "Since you're so helpful."

He embraced this chore, bustling back and forth between silverware drawer and table, making several trips.

Meg peeked into the dining room. He had set four places. "Oh," she said, "it's just us. He's already gone to get her. As discussed."

She brought the eggs and two plates to the table, passing him returning the extra silverware to the kitchen. "That's all right," she said. "You can leave it."

But he went anyway. She could hear the careful clinking of returning silver. Several minutes passed.

"Eggs are getting cold," she called into the kitchen. Surely he had already returned two forks and two knives, but there was more clinking of silverware.

What was he doing now, rearranging the drawer?

"Come on, have a seat," she called. "Right here." She slapped the table, mustering a little levity. "Right here's the best place to eat."

Finally he came back into the dining room.

"Sit. You've been an awful big help."

"She's going to be really mad that she has to come home," he said.

"Don't worry about her." Meg piled eggs on his plate.

"She hates having to do things because of me," he said.

Honey, she could have said. *It's not you; it's not your fault. Never think that.*

But she said nothing. Her palm smarted from smacking the table. She sat with him while he ate and ate, until the doorbell rang.

It was Ben Handke, his empty Caledonia County sheriff's car still running as he stood at the door. Meg was pleased, relieved, that the boy was eating a hearty breakfast in the dining room. *See, Ben, I am a good mother.*

"Meg," Ben said. He took off his hat and held it over his heart. He bowed his head.

"This isn't a wake," she said.

"How are things today?" His words, smoke dust in the cold, formed and fell visibly.

"Well, you did it, Ben. You got Jeff home."

He stamped his feet on the mat, the sound of men in winter. His getaway car, puffing away on the side of the road, revved a low idle, as if catching its breath. It had a rustic sheriff's star decalled on the driver's door, as if this were the Old West.

She had the urge to lay her face on his chest, his breath falling as mist into her hair, his overcoat imprinting a faint sheriff's-issue pattern on her cheek.

Instead, she invited him in, offered him coffee and some breakfast. "We have plenty. He's cooked at least half a dozen eggs."

"Jeff?"

"No, Charlie. Age eight and he's made me breakfast, thank you very much." *See how much the son loves the mother of this house.*

"He's not in school today?"

"Not today," she said, thinking fast. "This asthma." She clamped a hand over her chest, to indicate his fast-beating lungs, to cover up her fast-beating heart. "I'd like to make sure it's run its course. Nothing much'll be going on in school today, anyway, the Friday before vacation.

"How about it, Ben? Will you take some of this breakfast off our hands?"

He thanked her but declined.

"I know it smells a little *blackened* from here," she said, "cajun omelet, but we remedied that problem. He started the cooking, but I finished it off. I assure you, the results are pretty good."

"I don't doubt it," he said. "But I've eaten. Just stopping by to make sure everything's okay. Make sure Jeff got home all right, that he's been fully informed of yesterday's events. . ."

"About that, Ben," she started, not having any idea where she would go.

Her mind leapt to what *yesterday's events* should have been: At 3:40, the bus dropped off Charlie Carroll, who hopped into the mudroom while his mother stuck her head out the front door. He would de-jacket and de-boot, then come to sit in the kitchen with her, to get a head start on all the different ways he would not eat what she was cooking. Stew, let's see . . . You could mash vegetables against the bowl with the back of the spoon, cut the seitan into tiny pieces until it looked gone . . .

Or at 3:40, the bus dropped off *no* child in front of her house. Didn't go to school today, up in his bedroom, playing or reading or waiting or sleeping.

Either way, Meg might have crossed the lawn and talked to Sandy for a minute, about the generally improving weather, about the havoc mud wreaks on a bus's suspension, about how she should probably take down the plastic weatherstripping on some of the downstairs windows, let a little sun shine in. Maybe yesterday would have been the afternoon she invited him over for dinner after he dropped the bus off in the district lot behind the School Department. She had made plenty of stew—it had been simmering all afternoon and was enough for an army—and there was practically no one else to eat it. She didn't know why she still cooked for so many, she would say, chattering nervously, trying to cover her urge to touch him and see what happened.

"Let's not worry about that now," Ben said. "I wrote it up as *delay of county transportation*. That's all. But once something's in the System, I've got to follow up. You know how it is."

"Of course," she said, too emphatically for her own liking. "And here we are. Right as rain—or should I say mud—this morning. A little asthma, a little overcooked eggs. But a nice gesture on his part, I'll hasten to add."

"How about I say hello to Jeff, see how his drive was?"

"He'll tell you what he told me, Ben. Not a stitch of traffic. In fact, he made an eleven-hour drive in ten.—Oh, not that he was speeding, Officer."

"Good. Good. All the same . . ."

"He's not here. He's gone to pick up Katie, bring her home for spring break."

"How is she? How's that private school working for her—what is it, Green Mountain School?"

One time, *one time,* Meg had commingled Katie and the System. Because it was a small town, because a mother gets worried, because sometimes she has no one else to turn to for help. She had made one panicked call to the Sheriff's

Department, to Ben in particular, Jeff's softball teammate, when Katie had made arrangement after arrangement with friends in such a daisy chain that her mother—Jeff must have been away—could not keep up. *Sorry, she just left; nope, she's not here yet.* Eventually, a friend's mother called Meg, to make sure it was all right if Katie spent the night. Not without a giant lecture, Meg said, letting Katie know that she had called the police, that's how worried she was.

"Are you asking all this as the sheriff?" Meg said. "Or as a friend? As my husband's former softball teammate, as a concerned citizen? As another Vermont parent?"

"All of the above. As a friend, yes. But I also want you to know that the County, the State—the System—is here for you."

"Thank you," she said dryly.

A few years ago, there was a missing-child scare in Caledonia County, and the sheriff spoke to an assembly of parents. Meg could still picture him in the upper-school gym, enumerating steps a sheriff's department would take in such a case. There would be a BOLO alert—"Be On the Lookout"—issued to all units. A formal missing person's report, usually not filed until twenty-four to forty-eight hours from disappearance, was filed immediately for a child under twelve. Meantime, the family would be asked to compile an exhaustive list of anyone, *anyone*, who might know about the child, his habits, whereabouts, favorite places, secrets. Teachers, neighbors. Even shopkeepers in stores he frequented. Any new friends, any new teams or clubs that he'd joined lately? the parents would be asked. Any change in daily routines?

Joan Shearer would have had a field day with this. Meg could just imagine her neighbor inciting teachers, neighbors, shopkeepers: *Didn't a boy who looked an awful lot like her son get off the school bus—though not without some drama—at the end of the day?*

At that assembly, Ben had handed out a photocopied list of questions for which parents should have a working knowledge of the answers. Even if the child never goes missing. "Sometimes," he'd said, "by answering all these questions—in other words, by taking an interest in your child—you can prevent him or her from getting away from you in the first place." He urged parents to prepare a Law Enforcement Action File (LEAF) before it was needed, in the hopes that it never would be.

Ben had emphasized—as he had soon after, when Meg called worried about Katie—that children very rarely just disappear. More than 95 percent who go missing are found unharmed, in the hands of people they know, as was the child in the case that caused such a scare. That six-year-old girl had been taken by her mother, in the middle of a bitter custody battle, to a small town on the Maryland coast, sheltered, and given a new identity by a nationwide network of mothers who called themselves POOCH, Protectors of Our Children. This underground railroad acquired new school and fingerprint records, and helped a runaway parent, almost always a mother, change her and her child's appearance with dyed hair or wigs, new clothing styles and mannerisms, and red-herring characteristics such as an affected limp or stutter that might cause them to go unnoticed by BOLO alerts.

• • •

"I have something for you," Ben said. "For him, really." He ducked outside for a small black bag he had stashed on the stoop. He took out a Zip-Lock bag, from which he removed a muddy yellow scarf.

Meg gasped, covering her mouth so quickly she created a pocket of suction and couldn't breathe for a moment. Familiar, muddy, vestigial—this was how cops presented evidence from a murder.

"It was apparently wedged behind the backseat of the bus." Ben held out its fringed end so she could see the black lettering: Midas. It was a scarf Charlie had gotten at one of Katie's ski races, a promotional event a few winters ago.

"Sandy didn't know how long it's been there," he continued. "It could have been dropped anytime over the winter. Just thought I'd return it, since I was coming by anyway."

"Charlie!" she called. She shrugged to Ben. *I don't know what else to call him.*

He appeared in the hall archway. Reporting for duty.

Ben shook the scarf at him a little.

"He's not a dog," Meg said.

"Of course not," Ben said, offering up the scarf again but no longer shaking it. "Is this yours?"

The boy wrinkled his nose at the dirt-stiffened thing the sheriff was holding by two fingers.

Ben came inside and closed the door behind him, not taking his eye off the child. He seemed to be sizing the boy up, looking at his ears, his neck, any exposed skin, the way his clothes fit. He craned his own neck, as if he could see around or through the boy.

Did Ben see it, too? See that this was not her son?

"Come here, son," he said.

But how could Ben have known? He might have met Jeff's little boy at a softball game a few years ago, spoken to a group of third-graders at one of Union Valley Lower's safety assemblies, or seen Meg with the boy a time or two in town.

The boy took a few steps across the foyer, tentatively, as if Ben were going to snatch him up once he got close enough. Maybe that was the real purpose of this evidentiary enterprise—to take the boy. Hold him for the disappearance of Charlie Carroll.

"You all right?" Ben said. "You doing all right here at home with your mother?"

Wait! Ben was going to take the child for his own good. Get him away from the mother.

She stepped between them. "The scarf," she said quickly. "Tell the sheriff if it's yours, Chappy. If it's maybe that 'Midas muffler' they gave away at Katie's ski race a few years ago. If maybe you left it on the school bus, behind one of the seats."

"Yes," he said. "I'm pretty sure it is."

"There's your answer, Ben. Now, why don't I have Jeff give you a call when he gets back."

"Good . . ." Ben said distractedly, making no move to leave. "You'll be in school on Monday?"

"Yes," the boy said.

"See," she said. "Nothing to worry about, Ben."

"Are there more eggs?" the boy asked.

"On the stove."

"Besides that?"

"Besides the ones you cooked? Did you finish those?"

He nodded.

"My goodness," she said. "That's about six eggs you ate!"

He squinted. "Is that too many?"

"Not for an army."

"I'm not an army."

"Well, that's what I'm saying. It was a joke."

"I know," he said. "'I'm not an army' was a joke, too."

"Wait," Ben said. "Monday's District Thirty-two's vacation. No school Monday."

"*Next* Monday," the boy said.

"Exactly," Meg said. "We thought you meant next Monday. Of course you didn't mean this coming Monday. That's school vacation. Everyone knows that."

She turned to her son. "Why don't you go back into the kitchen and have some bread if you're so hungry." There was sweet anadama bread in the bread box, she told him, in addition to that tasteless high-protein stuff.

"He's always hungry," she said once he'd gone. "I hope the System knows that, Ben. He's just eaten six eggs. He'll eat the State out of house and home."

"Six eggs," Ben said, massaging the arteries in his chest. "That's an awful lot."

She had intended to prove herself a good mother by nourishing and caring for this boy. But instead, the sheriff was anxiously working the idea of six eggs' worth of cholesterol from his own heart and, no doubt, judging this mother a distant second to the System.

Ben put the yellow scarf back in the Zip-Lock bag and turned to leave. "We're on the same team, Meg," he said. "I'll do my job, and you do yours."

"*Mine?* That's a good one."

She would rather do his. His had procedure and evidence, the System and the State.

5

SLAMMING THE MUDROOM DOOR, Katie kicked off her Sorels, took dressy high-heeled loafers out of her bag, and screwed them on her feet. She must have borrowed the shoes; Meg did not recognize them. But she recognized Katie. At thirteen and furious, she still had the clear, hot skin of a child, while she stood with the awkwardness of a teenager in these new, tippy shoes. Taller each time they saw her, and ever more independent, but still *Katie*, lively, restless, angry, essentially Jeff's, and, at the same time, stuck with her mother for good.

"Quit staring at me," Katie said.

Meg imagined hugging her—*Hello, baby*—but knew she could not without her daughter snapping in half or going up in flames. "Thanks for coming home."

"Did I have a choice?" Katie said.

"You have a choice whether to be part of this family or not," Jeff said. "Like I told you in the car."

"Not yet I don't," she muttered. "Only *you* do."

Meg did a complicated eye maneuver to let Jeff know that the boy was up in Charlie's room, that nothing had changed from this morning, and that Katie should not be offered such a choice again.

Jeff must have played it down, the trouble that he'd consigned Charlie to. Katie was probably thinking it was just another bout of asthma or flu. Her brother was always coughing and wheezing. On top of that, he caught anything that blew through town. Why should *she* have to come home because of *him*?

"I'm going skiing starting on Sunday, you know, no matter what the crybaby has to say about anything."

"This is what I'm talking about," Meg said to Jeff. Then, to Katie, "It's a long time till Sunday."

Katie stomped her feet again, exaggerating them *planted*. "Here I am," she said. "Now what am I supposed to do?"

"Who are you, your father?" Meg said.

"Go talk to your brother," Jeff said.

"Where's the ninety-pound weakling?"

Meg gestured to the stairs with a resignation that, if Katie were anything other than thirteen, would have scared her but good.

Katie's clicking heels accompanied her through the house as though she had brought home a friend, someone from her new world to help fend off her hopelessly familiar family.

"Ninety pounds?" Meg said. "That would be nice."

By the time Meg arrived upstairs, Katie was standing,

staring, at the mouth of her brother's room. Meg could not watch. She shut her eyes, trying to convince herself that she was subjecting Katie for her own good. Like dipping a squirming child into a body of water for the first time, or delivering a sobbing child to the opening day of school. What feels like cruelty is not: you must make children safe on a planet that's 70 percent water, comfortable in a world they're sharing with six billion people.

"Hi," the boy said, sitting on the bed.

Katie brushed at her cheeks with her hands, narrowing her eyes. She kept replanting her high-heeled shoes for balance.

Meg felt closer to this polite, cheerful boy than to her teenage daughter, just back from private school and wearing someone else's shoes.

From the ground floor came the audible sounds of Jeff pacing. He had started behind Meg and Katie but stopped before the stairs. The rule—boots off at the door—was Jeff's to begin with, and Katie was the original rebel. Now, she wore dry inside-shoes while Jeff paced the living room and foyer in his Timberlands.

"You can come in," the boy said. "See what I got?"

Like a showman rather than a sick little boy, he gestured to his night table, arrayed with asthma paraphernalia now in festive disguise. The nebulizer was pushed to the back and draped with a T-shirt so it appeared mysterious rather than convalescent. He could whip off the cloth to reveal—ta-da!—what? The materials Charlie used for breathing exercises now looked like party decorations: a pack of not-yet-inflated balloons, two candles in the shapes of Gumby and Pokey, matches his mother let him use after he demonstrated a fear-of-God understanding of fire safety. Even the PANIC button looked benign, a funny red clown nose, the CANCEL switch above it a winking eye.

"So?" Katie said.

On the bus, Meg had found herself expecting that the boy would eventually shift the picture of their lives back into focus. She realized she was expecting the same from Katie. Climbing the stairs behind her daughter, she had been thinking that Katie would announce herself home—*thank you, thank you,* taking a bow—march right into her room, and shut the door.

Instead, she had done what she was told, went to talk to her brother. And, like an adult, simply absorbed what she saw. The moment of her arrival was like a spilled drop of mercury, balling up, gathering its toxicity unto itself.

"Hon, something's the matter," Meg whispered. "Something's wrong."

"Something's always the matter in this house."

"Please," Meg said. "Don't say that."

"*Please,*" Katie mimicked. "You got that from Dad. He always says it like it means something. You can have whole fights with Dad and all he ever says is *Please.*"

Meg clenched a fist. "Katie—"

"It's a fact. You can't yell at me about a fact."

"Listen, I'm just trying to have a *conversation* with you." She unclenched her hand, flexing it open and closed, open and closed.

"For your information, nobody calls me Katie anymore. It's *Katherine*."

"For *your* information, it's your parents who gave you that given name in the first place."

"Ashley and Rachel call me Kat."

Meg could see that she must be pursing her lips because Katie was mocking the gesture with her own mouth. The tighter Meg pressed her lips, the tighter Katie did. The higher Meg raised her index finger, the higher Katie waved hers.

Up and up and up, until sobs filled the hallway. Meg shuddered, thinking for an instant that Katie had split in two—one Katie, *Kat*, baiting and mocking, the other crying and crying.

No, it was him. Facedown on the bed. Gasping sobs traveled delayed from the bedroom like light from stars.

"See what you've—" Meg started.

"Me?" Katie looked right through her mother and went into Charlie's room.

The slamming door behind her was all that was familiar about this. Katie usually went the opposite direction when it came to him: getting up from the dinner table mid-meal, clearing her plate preemptively, when he tried to engage her in conversation; running from Charlie (actually *running*, losing him with the first step) when he tried to follow her or her friends. Or she would turn rotten-sweet—that smoky-saccharine *Hello, honey*, followed by *Now get out of Your Highness's room, please*. A phase that had made Meg miss the shoving-and-punching phase. It was so easy for Katie to push him around, literally, that she made things interesting for herself by turning the tables and imploring him to punch her in the arm. *Again, harder. Harder than that, weakling.* He would swing with all his might, raging with impotence, gritting his teeth, shaking his fist as if priming a pump. *Nope, still didn't hurt,* Katie would taunt. Until Meg would come in the room. "Katie, stop it. You're going to hurt him." Hurt *him*? Katie would know enough to know it, although she would protest, "Ma, *he's* the one punching *me.*" She would then pretend to hug him, while actually trying to squeeze the breath out of him.

Now, there was no taunting or punching audible from this side of the door, only mumbling, as if the children were actually having a conversation. Meg could hardly imagine what they were talking about, so separate were their worlds. *How's school? Good, how's your school? Good. How's your mom? Crazy, how's your mom?*

Then again, she'd never heard this boy talk to a teenage girl. Who knew what he'd spin to impress her? *And then I ran away from my wicked stepmother in, um, Canada, and I jumped on a train to Birchwood, Vermont, and then your brother, your real brother, died because he was sick. And there was an extra seat on the Union Valley Lower bus . . .*

Or did he somehow know a story that Charlie might tell? *Mom's hard to figure out. Sometimes she asks me a million times how I feel, if I'm sure I'm all right, and cooks me special foods that I don't like but I'm not supposed to anyway, it's just that they're high in protein and low in allergens. And sometimes she doesn't ask me or cook me anything at all, and sometimes she has to step outside*

*for a minute because the house is "a little too close," she says, even
though it's so big, but she always reminds me that I have a PANIC
button that can call the doctor and the police automatically anytime I
have to.*

The door swung open.

"Entrez, s'il vous plaît," Katie said, brushing by her
mother.

"Wait one minute, s'il vous plaît," Meg said.

Katie stopped at the top of the stairs. "I don't even live
here, you know."

"Oh, you most certainly do. Just because you're away at
private school from September to May does not mean that
you can walk away from me when I'm asking you a question."

"What question?"

Meg had thought the question—*Who is he?*—was obvious. "Come back up here."

"I am." Katie was two steps down.

"Up here. Right now."

"If you're going to ask me about him, save your breath. I
don't want to talk about it." She took two steps back
upstairs. "Can *I* ask *you* a question?"

"Yes. Please."

"Can I still go skiing on Sunday?"

"We'll have to see. First things first. First thing is to see
how he, how your brother, seems to be doing."

Katie rolled her eyes.

"Well?" Meg said.

"Weird," Katie said. "Okay? He seems to be doing really
weirdly."

She popped away and went down the stairs. "Like something, I don't know, *happened* to him," she called from the bottom.

Meg went back to Charlie's room. He was sitting on the bed, on the brink, she could tell, of crying again. She should have gone in and put her hand on his back—if not as comfort then at least as permission, as blessing. *It's okay, cry all you want.* That would have been a familiar ritual. Katie was right: Charlie was a crybaby.

Instead, she closed the door. They hardly knew each other.

She listened for the crying to be followed by a coughing fit, which never came—unless she couldn't hear well enough through the closed door. What a cruel thing a door is. It keeps you from the other side at the same time it lets you know full well that there *is* an other side. She listened to nothing for the longest time. Then, gradually, she made out a steady breathing, like you eventually see a star if you stare long enough at any one spot in a clear night sky. Breathing! Clear, steady breathing.

She held her breath in order to better hear his.

Again, nothing. What she had been hearing, it turned out, was herself. She had been pressed against the door so hopefully that her own breathing sounded, for a moment, like it was coming from the other side.

6

"ROUTINE, ALL ROUTINE," Dr. Ireland said as he felt the boy's glands, pressed his sternum, took a stethoscope and two fingers to his back and chest.

"Okay". . . *thump*. . . "normal". . . *thump*. . . "just fine."

Meg heard all this as a premonition of its opposite and waited for something out of the ordinary to happen. For the boy to float away, perhaps, when Dr. Ireland inflated the blood-pressure cuff around his arm. Or for the doctor to gasp in surprise as he shone his penlight into the boy's pupils. But the only surprise so far was utter normalcy.

"Anything funny going on in there?" the doctor asked, flattening the boy's tongue with a wooden depressor. "Anything I should know about?"

The boy tried to shake his head, but the doctor braced his chin. "No sudden moves, okay, cowboy?"

He squinted—in agreement or confusion?—best he could with his mouth pried open. Why would the doctor trick him like that, Meg wondered, ask a question then scold him for answering?

"What do *you* think, Frank?" Jeff plucked a tongue depressor from the stainless-steel cup on the counter and fiddled with it. "That's why we're here. To see what the trained professional has to say."

At Jeff's insistence, they were at Central Vermont Hospital, where Dr. Ireland had office hours Tuesdays, Thursdays, and every other Friday. The sheriff, the doctor. Trained professionals, with their evidence and answers. Meg supposed a funeral director would elicit Jeff's sorrow, a circus owner his glee. She also supposed that this emotion-by-office clarity was what drew her, a woman, to him, a man, in the first place.

"Childhood conditions can be impressionistic," Dr. Ireland said. "Often your best answers come down to what the family—the mother, usually—sees happening in the child, what works and what doesn't work."

"He's gotten a wonderful new appetite from somewhere," Meg said.

"That so?" the doctor said, running his fingers up and down the boy's ribs like piano keys.

"That *is* so," the boy said, chivalric as a son.

"How about those breathing exercises? And is he getting better with the inhaler?"

The boy brightened, his head filling with test answers. *So that's what all those things are for!* That little plastic thing that looks like a kazoo, those balloons, the candles . . . To breathe, of course!

"Good, then?" the doctor asked.

The boy, a sucker for expectation, nodded eagerly.

"Done," the doctor pronounced and slapped him on the back.

He screwed up his face, looking surprised and a little insulted, as if the pediatrician had been trying to knock him over.

"I have a good idea," the doctor said. "How about the adults go to my office and talk, and I'll call in my favorite patient's favorite nurse for some finishing touches? Dotting the T's and crossing the I's."

Meg noticed the boy playfully try to cross his eyes. Or it might have been a look of fear coming over him.

The favorite nurse burst into the room like a hostess and flicked the light switch on. "There, that's better," she said. "A little light on the subject."

The doctor had been conducting an exam in the dark? Meg wouldn't have thought so. In fact, now that the overhead lights had been turned on, the noonday room actually looked dimmer, yellower.

"Olivia," the nurse said, proffering her hand to Meg, Jeff.

"Yes, of course," Meg said, at the same time Jeff said, "Nice to meet you." He looked chagrined. An introduction: a reminder of how long it had been since he'd been to the doctor's with his son.

"Olivia, Olivia," the boy said under his breath, studiously. *Remember that, remember that . . .*

"Okay, then, if we leave you two to your own devices?" Dr. Ireland said.

"Fine with me," the favorite nurse said.

"Fine with me," the favorite patient repeated. The words caught in his throat, making his voice crack and embarrassing him. But he cleared his throat, tried again. "Fine," he said boldly. "I'm fine."

Good boy, letting the parents leave the room with a clear conscience.

File folder in hand, Dr. Ireland ushered them into his office. "Sit, sit," he said.

Meg and Jeff remained standing.

"All right, then," Frank said. "Why don't you tell me what you were expecting today, now that we're alone." He clapped the shoulder of the only child in the room—a hollowed-out bust propped on the edge of his desk. Expressionless and androgynous, the model had colored organs fitted like puzzle pieces in its abdomen cavity. Dr. Ireland had used it over the years to teach Charlie about lungs, why his felt the way they did, itchy and like they were closing sometimes. The doctor would remove the model lungs, give one to Charlie to hold, one to his mother. "Lungs are like sponges," he'd say, although these were hard, molded plastic.

"How about starting with what happened, when was it, Wednesday night? With the false alarm," the doctor said.

"What false alarm?" Jeff said. "What happened?" Then, to the doctor, "I've been out of town."

"The QuicKonnect unit rang through—" Frank started.

"What happened, Meg? Why didn't you tell me?"

"Another attack?" the doctor prompted.

"Not exactly," she said, stalling. "What does the file say, Frank?"

"I'd rather hear what you have to say," he said.

Jeff was spooling his hands *come on, come on.* He tried to still them by fiddling with the tongue depressor.

"Let's break it down to a few questions," Frank said. "What was happening with him when you pressed the QuicKonnect button? And what happened next? We have a note that the mother wasn't available to talk on the phone when our dispatcher followed up."

There it was, then. There was the record of Wednesday night, the night before the bus brought her another boy because she didn't deserve the one she had. "He started to," she started. "And he must have panicked. But in a minute, he was fine. One two three, he was fine. So we canceled."

"Are you sure?" Jeff said. "Did you talk with a dispatcher?"

She closed her eyes to try to find a cover story, but instead she trapped the image of him the other night, lying in bed with a faint red aureole by his head. He must have pressed the PANIC button to get someone's attention when he couldn't get hers. His coughing had now expired, and he was lying still, on his right side, the correct side, breathing so silently that he might not have been breathing at all. He never slept that quietly. The sleep of the dead. She reached around his night table and hit the CANCEL switch.

"Ouch!"

She opened her eyes to Jeff wincing, mouth open in

pain. He'd gotten a splinter in his hand from the tongue depressor.

"Your hand," Meg said. Finally, something was actually wrong in the doctor's office. "Let Frank take a look at that."

"It's nothing," he said, clamping his palm over his fist. *Rock, paper, scissors*. "And I mean *really* nothing. Let's not lose focus here of what's nothing and what's something."

"Jeff, we're in a *doctor's* office. For heaven's sakes, let him take out your splinter."

"She makes a good point," Dr. Ireland said, already preparing an antiseptic swab.

"I'm fine I'm fine I'm fine," he repeated as Meg and Frank both came at him. The doctor held up the hand. Splinter was barely visible beneath skin, like a coin underwater.

"I'll get it later," Jeff tried one more time before giving in.

He looked terribly uncomfortable, proud lion bearing his paw, and he betrayed no mounting pain as the doctor had to dig deeper and deeper under the skin. He tweezed it out and swabbed it with antiseptic.

"Good as new." He clapped a Band-Aid on Jeff's hand, closing a deal, then clapped together his great healing palms, which, if Meg wasn't mistaken, puffed dust like blackboard erasers.

"Now then," the doctor continued, "tell me why isn't he in school today? He seems, as the kids say, good to go."

"His sister's home," Meg said, "and his father. Family reunion of sorts. It was Jeff's idea. I had to agree. There's so little going on in school the Friday before vacation."

"Okay," Frank said. "But now may be a good time to start

changing course. It may be that he's gone and done it, grown out of the acute asthma stage. We've always known this was a real possibility. If so, no more babying him. 'Off to school, champ. No rest for the wicked.' Something like that.

"Which, I'll hasten to add, you should have been doing all along. But especially now, in a transition time. With him turning into a real Rough Rider." Teddy Roosevelt was a regular part of the doctor's repertoire. Famous asthmatic, famous bull moose.

"How long until we can call him cured?" Jeff asked.

"We prefer to call it remission," Frank said. "Asthma is still a chronic condition. But let's see—what was the date of the latest attack?" He paged through the folder. "Looks like we have to go back a while for the real deal. Back and back and back."

Back and back and back. To a night, any night, when she rushed into his room, his breathing sounding like sucking though a cracked straw. She would help him strap on the nebulizer as tears streamed down his face. Not tears of panic—he would tell her time and time again that he was not scared—but tears of imbalance, body fluids going haywire, nothing pooling or draining where or how it was supposed to. Disconcertingly, he got more color in his face during an asthma attack, turning from his everyday pale to a hyperventilated pink.

The other night, the night on file, was different. The coughing he woke her up with was exaggerated, suspiciously shallow, each cough dry and discrete and willful, not gaspy and enjambed.

"Any way to quantify how much better he is?" Jeff said. "With tests? The total serum IgE, or these new ones, leuko-cytoxicity tests? Some certainty would be nice."

"Jeff, no more needles," Meg said. "Maybe you've for-gotten—maybe you never knew—that he has small, closed veins. Do you know, Dr. Jekyll, how long it takes a nurse to raise a vein in him? How he sits there patiently, never cry-ing, which is so much worse than actually crying. The one place he won't cry is the doctor's office, and it breaks a par-ent's heart, a mother's, to watch him."

She pictured the latest incarnation of Nurse—this one, like the rest, thinking she was the favorite—tap-tapping two fingers against the silken inside of this boy's elbow, trying to raise a vein, making a game out of it, hide-and-seek with blood vessels, as Meg had seen them do before with Charlie.

All this to tell what she already knew. Then they would have to turn back to Ben, right office for the right job, to look in earnest for Charlie Carroll, now almost twenty-four hours gone. They would search cold trails, the plentiful woods in the constantly shifting light. The reinsulated attic, the barn, the basement woodshop, all off-limits to him with their fiberglass dust, fumes, wood shavings. So many haz-ards, so many places to disappear, right in their own home. Even right in his oversized bedroom, floor X'ed-off like a giant, lying-down grave marker.

"How about testing *us*, Jeff," she said. "You and me—see how well the parents know the child? Does he sleep better with the light on or off, your son? What games does he like? What does he want more than anything else in the world?"

"Please," Jeff said. "Let's not do this here."

"Where, then? What would be a better place? The house? Even when you're home, I can barely find you. Why not here? At least I know where you are."

"Asthma, any childhood condition, really, can persist stubbornly without answers, I'm afraid," the doctor interjected. "Sometimes the best we can do is trust the primary caregiver's intuition."

If only the doctor, Jeff's great arbiter, could come live in their house: a standing adjudication amid two parents' standing differences.

A blast of cold air came from a vent in the ceiling. She pictured the boy in his underwear next door. Healthy though he was, the poor thing must be cold, half naked like that.

"Frank, does this seem like Charlie to you?" Jeff blurted. "Is this Charlie?"

Frank smiled. "I know what you mean," he said. "For now, let's focus on the fact that he's getting better."

"He's better, Meg," Jeff said. "This is what we've been waiting for."

No more going to Charlie's room every five minutes, bearing a thermometer, more steroids for the nebulizer or beta agonist for the inhaler, two hopeful slices of dry protein toast or room-temperature ginger ale for an upset stomach, comic books and word searches for a lonely boy. No more navigating a fine line between making him better and making him worse: relax the bronchi too little and he can't breathe, too much and the walls of the airways can come tumbling down. Too much cortisone or too little . . . too much attention or too little . . .

"Onward and upward," the doctor said. "Remember the Alamo!" He punctuated his charge with a slap on the back for the hale child model. Plastic parts shifted and settled.

What if this, the eraser-colored child with visible pastel organs, had been the child who arrived on the bus? She could have watched the heart when she invited him into the house, watched for a lifting or a sinking. She could have tracked the vegetable stew to see how the stomach accepted helping after helping, rather than the familiar "digestive interruption." She could have seen quite clearly the state of the lungs, that the bronchi remained free of asthmatic spasm. In fact, they were rock hard.

Meg plucked a lung from the chest cavity. "Why use this as an example, Frank?" she said. "It's much too hard. Why use this to explain exactly the opposite—why his lungs *shouldn't* feel hard and unforgiving?"

"You're missing Frank's point," Jeff said, "which is that in his medical opinion, Charlie's getting better. I appreciate the fact that things once were difficult, but—"

"Once? How about hundreds of times? How about just the other night? How about this very morning, earlier, when you went to pick up Katie and it was just me and him again?"

"These childhood conditions are nobody's fault." Frank's familiar gambit.

Jeff was compulsively tracing his Band-Aid with a finger, as though he had to keep drawing its outline or the thing would disappear. He would have been pacing if there had been more space in this cramped office. "This isn't anyone's fault," he echoed. "The doctor just said it was no one's fault."

"Maybe it *is*," she said, the lung's weight satisfying in her hand.

"Whose, mine?" Jeff said. "You want to hear that it's my fault—that I'm never home, that I want him to toughen up a little? Or yours? Do you want to hold yourself responsible for something that you couldn't possibly—"

She threw the lung across the room. "His," she said. "Maybe it's Charlie's fault."

She'd expected the lung to be much more brittle, to shatter or at least break in two, but it bounced several times before rocking to rest unharmed. She shook the whole damn child by its armless shoulders. It gave at the wrong places—not at the joints, but at the organs. The remaining lung fell to the floor, and the tumbling heart, followed by the rest of the viscera. Stomach, intestines, liver, pancreas, kidneys.

"That's more like it," she said.

She left the room to the faint clicking of the doctor and Jeff refilling the child's abdomen cavity.

"Now cough for me," said Nurse Olivia.

She heard it again, that cued, fake cough, strong and show-offy, dry and in control.

"Mom," he called. He'd caught sight of her. "In here."

She hurried past the half-open door, as she had the other night, rushing by Charlie's night-lit doorway, down the hall to the stairs, down the stairs to the front door.

This time she had actual red EXIT signs to follow, which she did, down the corridor until she EXITED into the waiting room. And into relief at the familiar sight of her daughter, sitting and stewing, reading—no, manhandling—a magazine.

"What are you doing, miss?" A welcome opportunity to discipline.

Girls come under a centripetal force, stitched to the cycle by biology. Boys, boys are spun from mothers with centrifugal force, sent flying into the world. Meg thought her children had gotten this backward, but no. Look. Here was Katie, slumped in a chair nailed in a row, fixed to the floor. And on the other side of the red EXIT sign was a redheaded stranger who might right now be floating away, inflated by a blood pressure cuff, if he even existed in the first place.

"Nothing." Katie, busy breaking the back of a *Highlights* magazine, did not look up.

"I have eyes. Don't say *nothing* when I can see *something* perfectly well."

"Then why do you ask?" Katie said. "Besides, it's from October. So who the hell cares?"

"And I have ears. So don't use that language with me."

"'October'?"

Meg couldn't help a little laugh and flopped into a chair. Katie cracked a smile.

"One more thing I have," Meg said, "is a nose. Have you been smoking?"

Katie shook her head and pushed away the magazine, which left a trail of ash.

"You're lighting magazines on fire in a hospital, for heaven's sakes? Are you crazy?"

"No," Katie said. "Are *you*?"

"Maybe," Meg said. "But first things first. Fire is serious business. This is very dangerous. And in a hospital, where they have compressed oxygen and a million other things that could shoot up in flames."

"I hate hospitals."

She tried to remember what Katie, the healthy child, went to the pediatrician for: earaches, chicken pox, a nail in her heel from playing barefoot in the woods, a broken arm from gymnastics and later the same year a compensatory broken wrist. What they came home with: antibiotics, Dimetapp, bandages with dressing, a cast then a splint. *Lucky stiff*, according to Charlie, who revered his sister even further, if that was possible, because she got to have a cast *and* a splint and he never got to have anything but shots.

Katie turned back to her *Highlights*. "Goofus and Gallant," she said. "Gee, kids, they look exactly alike, but one of them does good things and one of them does bad things. Take your pick."

She looked up at her mother with a sarcastic smile. "Like anyone you know?"

Meg flushed, her breath already shallow, and quickly flipped the page. Better: a puzzle that featured disembodied, everyday items—sock, pencil, hammer—floating in a tree.

"What kind of moron couldn't find these things?" Katie said.

Meg pointed to a shoe in the tree and said, "Shoe."

Katie pointed to a wrench. "Wrench."

The two of them pointed and called out—stocking hat! pipe! moustache!—until they ran out of items on the page. Then they named items in the waiting room.

Clock.

Painting.

Sign that says Have your insurance information ready.

Coat rack.

Dad.

Jeff stood in the waiting room doorway.

Meg sharpened in her chair.

"Let's go," was all he said.

Katie hopped up and followed him out, leaving Meg to wait for the boy by herself.

To wait and wonder. What had Frank told Jeff? Not the answers to the questions she had asked him: Charlie cannot fall asleep with the light on, but when he wakes up coughing, he needs it on for the remainder of the night. No rest for the weary (Frank had it partially right). As for games, he likes word searches best, because you can do them alone. And what does he want more than anything else—besides his father? A pet, a dog. But, of course, the asthma.

What else did Frank have in his file? Surely QuicKonnect had not seen her at the front door, holding on to the knob for the longest time without turning it, trying to distract herself, to keep herself in the house by inventorying, say, all the weatherstripping she could see from here. Mortite caulking along the door. The coughing was fading, using itself up. Heavy sealing tape bordering the picture window. A few little syncopated coughs left. The one side window, old and rattly, covered in a plastic sheet stretched taut and affixed with a blow dryer. Finally, silence.

"Mom, didn't you see me?"

Here in this waiting room, his face the pink of health.

"You walked right by me. I was in the examining room."

Go get them! she had the urge to say. Jeff, Katie at his heel, would be outside now, crossing the parking lot. *Quick quick, before they drive away.* After a brief detour to drop Katie off at GMS for her ski trip, Jeff could be on his way back to Toronto. This boy could still catch them if he hurried.

"He's good to go," the nurse said. "The doctor told me to tell you that."

Meg asked if she could have a word with Dr. Ireland.

"I'm sorry, dear," said the all-of-twenty-year-old nurse, "the doctor's in with another patient now."

"I'd like to know what we should do for follow-up," she tried.

"I'm sure he'll call you with any necessary follow-up. That's standard procedure. Don't worry."

7

"MY FAMOUS APPLE CAKE," Joan Shearer said. "I'm sure it'll be all right for him. No sugar, no dairy. All natural, all delicious."

Meg put the Saran-wrapped tin on the plant stand and half expected the whole thing to come crashing to the floor. The cake was cast-iron heavy, with condolence and with what Meg was sure were holier-than-thou ingredients — organic apples, wheat flour, fruit juice.

"In a time like this," offered her neighbor, "I thought you could use a little sweet. I like to provide comfort when I can." She was shifting, searching over Meg's shoulder with enough curiosity to make Meg turn around.

There he was again, at the foot of the stairs. He shimmered in a shallow pool of familiarity. Even that argyle sweater was growing more familiar. After all, she had now laid eyes on him, and it, countless times in this house.

"Look," she said. "Mrs. Shearer brought us apple cake.

Remember how I was just saying that we had no apple cake in the house."

"I remember," he said, joining them in the foyer proper. "You said you hoped maybe somebody would bring us some."

"And now they have," she said.

"And now they have," he agreed.

"Raise the flag," she said.

"Raise the flag," he echoed.

"Isn't apple cake your favorite?" she said.

"My very favorite."

"Well . . . ?" Joan Shearer said, open-ended, clearly hoping to be let in the house, to be called in as some sort of confidante.

Meg tried to station herself between her ogling neighbor and the boy. But whenever she, Meg, moved, he moved as well, reading choreography into everything she did.

Joan's snooping was exacerbated by an oculomotor disorder that rendered her eyeballs fixed. Like the tight-socketed owl, minus the 270-degree head rotation and reputation for wisdom. To move her eyes, she had to move her head or even her body; she could not just sneak a peek.

"I thought it might be good for you to see a familiar face right now," Joan went on, leaning into the door as far as she could without an invitation. "Maybe my boys can stop by after school. If I can pry them away from that chemistry set Allen bought them for Christmas. They've attached themselves to it at the hip."

"What a nice sentiment." Meg could hear in her own voice where Katie must have gotten the idea that you could put saccharinity over on people.

Meg and Joan had been friends when the Landry-Carrolls moved to Vermont seven years ago. Mostly, they were friends out of proximity, as happens in sparsely populated places. They had kids around the same age and they were both home all day. Joan's company, her bottomless consolation, were welcome at first, but slowly Meg sensed that her neighbor was preying on her difficulties, which she loooved to hear about. *Oh, you poor thing, what happened next? Tell me more, tell me more.* And Meg did. She lamented Charlie's staying home from school day after day, and his inability to sleep through the night, night after night. *There but for the grace of God*, Joan would say. *You and your poor husband.* Not married, Meg reminded her.

"I notice that your . . . that Jeff's back." Joan nodded to the driveway. "But he's off again?"

I don't know how you do it. My Allen comes home from work and marches right into his red chair, where he'll be until bed. I take to that kind of predictability.

"He's just gone into town," Meg said. "He'll be right back." After the doctor's office, Jeff hadn't said a word except, when he stopped at the house, "Katie, come with me." He had been making a list of errands in the short time since he arrived: WD-40 for the doors; batteries for the smoke alarm; touch-up for the scratch in the plant stand where she'd been tossing her keys since Jeff and his household admonitions had hit the road.

"What are they doing in town again?" the boy interjected. "You might have told me, but I forgot."

This was something he could have figured out—*the father is always at the hardware store*—rather than fanning suspicion in front of Joan Shearer. "The hardware store, remember?"

Her brusqueness was enough to send him backing to the foot of the stairs, retreating as shyly as he had advanced. The shimmery sense of familiarity evaporated.

"Men and their habits," Joan Shearer said. "With my Allen, it's the bookstore. Come heaven or high water, he's got to make his stop at the bookstore."

Stuck in Meg's head was an imitation that Sandy did of Allen Shearer—holding his breath until his face turned red, then waving his hands around like a castaway trying to get the attention of an overhead plane. Sandy called him Mighty Mouse, following a fight the Shearers waged last year to alter the bus route so their sons, the second-to-last stop, could have more time after school to prepare for the Northern New England Apprentice Scientist competition. The Shearers had tried to enlist the Landry-Carroll family—Meg, that is—in the battle, but, given where they lived, Meg did not exactly see a way around a long bus ride, coming or going. Neither did she want anyone looking too closely at Charlie's school attendance.

"Even my little apprentice scientists have their needs," Joan went on. "'The pharmacy, the pharmacy.'" She whined in imitation, but proudly, boastfully so. "They like to see what they can combine to alter something-or-other's chemical makeup. My boys are curious as cats."

From Meg's boy, if she wasn't mistaken, came a low mewing sound. If she turned and looked at him right now, he would win her over for good. She kept her full-body focus on Joan Shearer, as if *she*, Meg, had an oculomotor disorder. A little playful cat noise might have been all it took for her to forget about Charlie.

"What about you, Charlie?" Joan said. "Are you a curious little boy?"

"Ask my mom," he said.

"Here, Curious George," Meg said, handing him the dead-weight apple cake. "Go take this into the kitchen. Cut yourself a piece."

"Since it's my favorite?" He raised his eyebrows and opened his face, inviting a game.

"Exactly," she said. "You can have two slices, since you've been so good."

When he left, Joan Shearer asked, "Why isn't he in school today?"

Meg invoked the "everyone's at home today" and "nothing much happens on vacation Friday" excuses again. But this was becoming an excellent question. Why wasn't he in school? What if she *had* sent him? She pictured him baffled at a musical-chairs attendance, Charlie's desk already occupied—by Charlie. Or perhaps this quick little one would sneak into the chair first, before the rightful owner. That's what Jeff was afraid of, anyway, that Charlie would be outpaced by other kids. Jeff wanted to toughen him up, send him into the battlefield of the playground, into the minefield of meat and chicken and fish. He's got to keep up with the world, Jeff would say. *But he's only six . . . seven . . . eight . . .*

From her Pandora's box of possibilities came another image: the teacher welcoming this new boy with much fanfare, trying to distract a class of eight- and nine-year-olds from the cloud of tragedy hanging over Charlie's empty seat. *Sit, sit, right here in this chair.* She'd slap the desktop, as Meg had the dining room table, both of them trying to right the situation like you whack a television picture clear. This boy would sit down, fold his hands on the desk, and hope for the best. He would not know that they were studying the Arctic, learning to count to ten in Russian (a different language the first Friday of each month), and dipping Easter eggs in art class. But he could fake it—no, *learn*—as well as the next kid.

- Seals guard against the cold with all that fat— poke, poke—which is like a down coat.
- Repeat after me: *ahdeen, dva, tree, chiteree, pyat, shest, siem, ochem, devyat, desyat.*
- Please pass the red dye. And the blue. I'm making my sister's favorite color.

"He's eager to spend time with his father and his sister, so I let him get a head start on vacation," Meg said.

"Don't let my boys get wind of that. I had to push them out the door this morning. They can't wait until vacation. They're going to science camp in Burlington. Science whizzes from all across the state. It's a nice challenge for them, not to be the smartest one in the room for a change."

Meg remembered anew why they'd stopped being friends.

The heave and rumble of an approaching heavy vehicle squashed the conversation flat.

"What on earth?" Joan said.

"Maybe they're regrading the road," Meg said, though she hoped it was what it sounded like: the school bus.

It had not made its usual stop at the house this morning.

Sandy had honored her request. Thank God she hadn't had to open the door at six-thirty in the morning again and give another go-on wave, dropping a quarantine pall over the place, or walk out to the bus to explain herself.

But now she welcomed a visit from Sandy.

The two women waited in the doorway to see what was coming. To watch the road with her oculomotor condition, Joan Shearer had to turn away from Meg completely. She could not split her attention as Meg could, able eyes darting from inside to outside, doorway to horizon, then back to her own feet to see if she was leaving or staying put.

It wasn't the school bus, but it *was* Sandy. On his tractor. He stopped just before the house, as if the lumbering tractor had to catch its breath.

"What does the bus driver want in the middle of the day?" Joan said.

"Joan, you'll have to excuse me."

Joan Shearer backed off the stoop in slow motion. She had not even been invited in, and here she was being sent home. She had failed to get any clues, and it had cost her an apple cake.

"If you could just return the tin," she said. "When you're done. You take all the time you need. Lord knows, I can wait."

•   •   •

Lord knows, Sandy Tadaveski could wait, too. Neither a school bus nor a tractor was likely to steal away to Toronto.

He did not get down off the tractor until Joan Shearer

had disappeared up the street, which took quite a while. She kept a tentativeness in her step, actually spinning around a few times (she could not simply glance back over her shoulder), to let her neighbor with the mystery know she would gladly come back anytime.

"Mom?"

She turned around. He looked like the cat that ate the canary, smacking his crumby lips.

"That apple cake tastes awful," he said.

"That's because it's good for you."

"I'd rather have a plain apple if I had to have something good for me."

"Touché," she said.

"What does that mean?"

She mimed the waving of a sword. He didn't seem to understand. "It means good job," she said.

She asked him to go upstairs, to wait there, because she had private things to discuss with Mr. Tadaveski. This was in part because she *did* have private things to discuss with Mr. Tadaveski and in part because she wanted to make the first disciplinary move, for a change. He had been sending himself upstairs regularly.

"You can come down when we're through talking," she said. "It's just that—"

"That's quite okay." He handed her the entire adult phrase and headed upstairs with what appeared to be a salute, although he might have been brushing hair off his forehead.

"Chappy," she called.

He turned around and ducked so she could see him beneath the bulkhead of the second floor. Then she saw a game dawn on him. He pressed his head up under the bulkhead, flattening his hair into a fringe. The game: holding up the house with your head.

"Just a minute," she said sternly. This game was not something she would ordinarily scold for. But the bigger game—she had not yet scolded him for that.

"Do you know why we call you Chappy?" she asked.

He fixed her with a serious, eager look that said: Isn't it enough that I'm holding up the whole house on my head?

When Charlie was a diaper-bottomed toddler, walking duck-footed and wobbly, Jeff started calling him Charlie Chaplin. Chappy for short.

"You don't know," she said.

"I think no one ever told me."

"Go upstairs and change your clothes," she said. "And *really* change them this time."

Outside, Sandy Tadaveski shuffled his feet like a throat-clearing. His face was a welcome sight, its Polish pleasantness, its understated palette—sandy, graying hair and fairly matching sandy-gray eyes, which looked like a brook you could see to the bottom of. Simple and accessible, clear and honest.

"Sandy, come in," she said. "Why does everyone stop right there on the stoop these days?"

"How is everything?"

"—and ask me that question?"

"You've been getting a lot of visitors?"

"Yes," she said. "Mostly my own family."

"How is he?" Sandy said.

Had they told Charlie where his nickname came from? Meg vaguely remembered believing that it was Jeff's story to tell if he wanted. His movie icon, his nickname. But Meg could not picture Jeff sitting down and telling this story— any story—to Charlie. Maybe Charlie *had* never heard the story. In fact, Katie probably did not know the origin of her nickname, either. Come to think of it, Meg could not be sure herself why they started calling Katie "Bear." Was it because she had once been soft and cuddly like a teddy bear? Or ferociously stubborn and territorial like a grizzly? Or had there been any reason at all? Perhaps the parents' mouths simply formed around the word when they opened them to talk to or about their baby daughter.

"Meg?" Sandy prompted. "How is everything?" He lowered his voice. "How's Charlie?"

"That's the question of the hour," she said. "And everyone asks like you do, all hushed like that. Ben, Joan Shearer. Even Jeff, to some degree. Can't meet my eye. Well, he's fine. One of the finest boys I've ever seen, really. It's just that he's not—oh, God, how many times will I have to say this?"

"I know." Sandy's voice was like a shade lowering around them.

"The strangest thing," she said, "is that he seems less strange every time I see him. He comes downstairs, and I think, I've seen this child come downstairs before. He comes into the kitchen, and I think, I've seen this child in the kitchen before. What's starting to scare me is how easy it would be to give in, to take it back. Just start calling him Charlie. As in, 'Charlie, go say good-bye to your father.'"

"What does Jeff have to say?"

"Oh, Jeff. Pretty much how it's always been: 'You're the mother, you know what's best.'"

"Do you?"

She took hold of Sandy's arm, its bicep beating like a heart, or a captive bird, under his windbreaker. Another one—she still had his jacket from yesterday.

He reached to touch her face.

But she stopped him with hospitality. "I'll tell you what's best," she said. "Your coming inside. What's really starting to scare me is everyone stopping outside like that." She banged her foot on the doorsill. "Damn doorway. Come in, Sandy, or I'll drag you in."

She led him into the living room. He, like everyone else who came in the house, seemed reluctant to sit down.

"Nice house," he said.

"Hard to heat."

"That's Vermont for you."

He looked around the room, although he tried to disguise his curiosity as shaking off the cold.

"They're at the hardware store," she said. "Everyone's at the hardware store but me and him. Just the two of us again."

"The three of us," Sandy dared.

Footsteps overhead broke the spell. "He's right upstairs," she said.

"So, I understand Ben's been by," Sandy said, back to business.

"You've been talking to him, too, I happen to know."

"He's been wondering about things, naturally. So I've cooperated. We're trained to. All school officials are, including transportation personnel. It's a whole industry, a whole horrible industry. 'Child safety,' they call it, though they mean 'child danger.'"

"What about that scarf?" Meg said. "Ben was over here yesterday with it."

"Ben wanted anything I found on the bus. Pretty slim pickings, really. I do a walk-through at the end of every day. I can usually match 'lost' directly with 'found' the next morning. Seeing the kids every day, I tend to know what belongs to who. That scarf, though, that was pretty well hid. It was really wedged in there."

"All his staying out of school, did you tell Ben about that?"

"No. That's up to you and Jeff."

"Of course he could check the school records if he wanted." She felt the undertow of exhaustion again. There was so much Ben could check if he wanted, so many records of a child, and so inexact. Even Jeff's recollections—which, given how his mind worked, could be taken as records—had little to do with Charlie as he had been over the last year, alone in the big house with a lonely mother, a mother who is waiting not so patiently for him to grow up at the same time that she is keeping him too young, who is scolding him out of the house for some fresh air at the same time she is letting him stay home from school because he says, day after day, that he doesn't feel well.

"There is something else," Sandy said. He held out Charlie's inhaler. "I found this on the bus, under the backseat near where the scarf was. I thought I'd tell you before I told Ben."

This wasn't the first time he'd found the inhaler on the bus, he explained. Charlie often tried to "forget" it, shoving it behind the seat, but Sandy would return it to him the next morning. Sandy had never said anything before; he must have assumed Meg knew, that of course a mother would notice if her asthmatic child came home from school without his inhaler.

Sandy handed it over, his hand lingering on hers in the process. Was this why he had possession of the inhaler in the first place? She tried to focus not on Sandy but on the beige object whose properties lay somewhere between plastic and magic. You could fit it in your palm; you could stick it in a backpack; it could save your child's life. Something of Charlie's to hold on to. Literally. She put it in her cardigan pocket and kept her hand on it, safety precaution turned talisman.

"Don't worry," Sandy said. "I'm on your side."

She leaned forward in her chair. Exhaustion was a constant undertow now.

"Meg. Meg."

She opened her eyes.

"Where'd you go?" Sandy stood and cupped a hand on the crown of her head, as if she were a child.

"What? I must have drifted off. I can't remember when I last slept."

"Poor girl." He ran his hand to her cheek.

"Careful," she said. "I could fall asleep in the palm of your hand."

"Why haven't you slept?"

"Last night, I was up all night waiting for Jeff. Playing and replaying the afternoon in my head. Then, the night before . . ." She blinked heavily. She could hear Frank's voice: *No rest for the wicked.*

"Seems so long ago," she continued. "The night before yesterday. Before you came by at the end of the school day with quite a surprise, to say the least."

Commotion in the mudroom. Meg and Sandy drew away from each other, magnetic poles suddenly switched. The boy was here too, halfway down the stairs. How long had he been there?

"Hey, Charlie." Sandy couldn't seem to help himself. He winked at the boy leaning on the railing, mid-staircase.

He had gotten out of that sweater at last. He was wearing a gray "Vermont" sweatshirt, drawstring puckering the neck, sleeves creeping up his forearms. Finally, Meg thought. Finally the worn-out thing was too small for anyone in the family. It had gone from Katie (a prized present-of-an-afternoon from Jeff) to Charlie with the usual negotiation and bribe: *It doesn't fit you anymore, miss. Let it be his favorite now. We'll buy you a new top . . . then get something pink and frilly that he won't want to wear. (No, he won't.)* Charlie had finished what Katie started, wearing it to threads. Come to think of it, Meg remembered getting rid of it, its days as a sweatshirt, as an actual piece of clothing, now over. She could have sworn she had ripped it in half then in half again, for the rag bag.

Meg scratched at her wrists, her hairline, suddenly feeling everyone where her skin was thinnest.

"Sandy," she whispered, "where does Charlie sit on the bus?"

"The back," he said, matching her conspiratorial tone. "All the boys want to sit in the back, but I give him first pick since he's on longest."

"In the backseat you can watch mud spray up behind the tires," the boy piped up.

When he stood up straight, Meg saw that not only had the sweatshirt not been quartered but it was not even too small. It had simply bunched up when he leaned over the railing. He pinched the shoulders into place, and the sweatshirt fit him again. He looked no more and no less like Charlie than he had earlier. He simply looked more casual.

"We missed you on the bus this morning," Sandy said.

"I'm kind of sick." He coughed twice, faking, then stopped.

Coughing *should* be finite, should be fake in an eight-year-old boy, she reminded herself, rather than prolonged to such a degree that mother and child wonder, each time, if he will ever stop.

"I hope you feel better soon," Sandy said.

"It's just a little cold," the boy said. "I don't have a fever or anything. I could probably go to school, but she doesn't think it's a good idea. Right?"

Meg unfocused her eyes to blur him sick. He kept snapping back fine.

"Right?" he pressed.

Fine, and not Charlie.

"Yes, right," she said.

From the mudroom, Katie was scolding Jeff to take off his boots. He was making excuses. The floors were cold. There was company. He was going right back out, anyway.

"I should go," Sandy said to Meg. "Let you get back to your family."

"At least let me give you your coat back."

"Give it to me later," he whispered. "I'd rather not see Jeff right now, while I'm coveting his wife."

She shot a look over to the boy to see if he registered her blush. She looked back in time to see Sandy shutting the door behind him.

8

IT WAS ALMOST TWO in the afternoon by the time Meg remembered that a family should eat lunch. When had they last been that, a family that ate lunch together?

The boy did not come downstairs when called, which sent Meg upstairs in a hurry. She had already come to expect he would show up for each meal, ready to eat.

He was not in Charlie's room. She knocked on Katie's door.

"What?" Katie said. "Can't a person have twenty-five seconds alone in this house?"

"Is anyone in there with you?"

"Like who? Your dream child?"

Meg noticed the closed bathroom door at the other end of the hall.

"Jeff?" she called, rushing down the hall.

"What?" Jeff answered from downstairs.

Charlie always left the door open, even a crack in the bathroom, as if he might be forgotten, left behind. She raised a hand to the door but did not knock. She stroked it like a child's back.

"Hon," she said, her lips so close to the door that she tasted wood. "Are you all right? What are you doing?"

Answer: running water.

"Are you all right?" she said. "Can I come in?"

She thought she could hear him through cascading water, but she couldn't make out what he was saying. It sounded like chanting, incanting. Maybe he was casting a spell, or trying to reverse one. Meg envisioned the sink filling with water. She envisioned the underside of a wrist, like skim milk to begin with, soaking and softening.

Jeff's touch on her back made her jump.

"What is it?" he said.

"He won't come out."

Jeff tried the door handle. "Damn. Stuck."

"He must have locked it."

"This lock hasn't worked for years," Jeff said. "Unless someone fixed it while I was away."

He must have jury-rigged something, the smart, desperate boy.

"Katie," Jeff called. "Come out here."

"You mean, *Katherine*?"

"Katie!" Meg echoed. "Your father said come out here this minute."

Stomping out of her room. "What's so wrong with the little creep now?"

"*All* the way over here, please," Jeff clarified.

Nothing doing. Katie had opened the door to the hallway linen closet and was using it as a shield, hiding behind it the best she could.

Jeff rattled the bathroom door handle again. "Too much paint on the hinges. This old house." He fingered the door seam. "I'll get a scraper."

The situation could have used a little more of the father's anger, for the boy's sake. But Jeff was already distracted, sniffing at the air like a mastiff.

"Is that smoke?" he said.

Smoke. *That's* what it was. When Katie first came out of her room, Meg had sensed something in the air, but she'd taken it to be the smell of anger.

"Were you smoking?" Jeff said.

"Oh, *please*," Katie said and retreated further behind the linen closet door. Floor-to-ceiling shelving was the only thing preventing her from crawling inside.

Meg turned back to the bathroom and banged on the door. "If he has to come back up here with a scraper . . ." She banged a few more times. "If he has to take this door off its hinges, someone will be very sorry." She kicked the bottom of the door.

"Meg, please," Jeff said, taking her by the shoulder. "You're scaring people."

But it worked. The bathroom door swung open.

Yet another boy.

Completely bald.

Red hair rimmed the sink basin; Jeff's razor lay in guilty repose on the counter. Meg gasped for everyone at the sight of the bright white skull.

"Now you can tell people I'm sick," he said. "You can tell them I have cancer or something."

Words are only words, Meg assured herself. Uttering cancer doesn't give you cancer. He didn't have cancer any more than he'd slit his wrists. He shaved his head. That was all. See: the razor, a sign of volition. No matter what he just said. And draining the faucet of water does not drain the body of blood.

He rubbed his hand over his head.

Meg couldn't take her eyes off him.

"Like when I was a baby," he said. "Remember when I was born? I had no hair. Remember?" *See, I remember now. I remember when I was a baby.* "You used to call me Baldy, remember?"

"*All* babies are bald," Katie piped up. "Who do you think you are, anyway?"

"Shhh," Meg said, putting her hand on her daughter's head, familiar, hot, full of thick hair. "Sometimes you whisper things to a baby that no one else hears."

At lunch, he kept running his hand over his head. He looked at once overgrown and too tender. Katie played with the ends of her hair and snuck glances at him.

"Katie," Jeff said. "Eat, please."

"Okay, Dad," she said, nicely for a change, seeming to be hypnotized by the glow of scalp at the table. She dug into her tomato macaroni and cheese, completely forgetting to disobey her father.

There was a knock at the door, a car running out front.

"Now who?" Meg said.

A second knock came with some urgency.

"I'll get it," Jeff said, and he left the room.

Please, let Jeff save the day.

"Maybe it's the sheriff," Meg said. "To arrest someone for underage baldness."

The boy smiled down to the table. He caught his reflection in a pot lid, which ironed the smile right off him.

The knocking continued. Finally, Meg went to the door. It was Ben. Jeff was nowhere to be found.

"Everything all right here?" Ben said.

"Not *everything*," Meg said. "Have you seen Jeff? I thought he was getting the door."

Ben shook his head.

"The amazing disappearing Landry-Carroll family," she muttered.

"How's Charlie?"

"Great!" she said, so enthusiastically that she must have sounded sarcastic. But she meant it. The boy was nothing if not great. Polite, strong, easygoing, funny. It's just that he was not—

"And your daughter? How's she?"

"Katie? You want her?"

Ben smiled warily.

"I'm joking, Ben. She's fine—for a teenager. She's tough. In both senses of the word."

"You don't feel like anyone's in danger, do you?"

"Danger? Should I?"

Now that the sheriff had introduced the word into the house, she could see danger everywhere. Starting right here in the doorway—between the storm door, which Ben held open with a planted foot, and the main door. There was danger in that threshold, whose crossing could spell the difference between inside and outside, together and alone, past and future. Between the son she had known for eight years and another boy who was equally as happy to disembark the school bus and hop inside after she'd let him know that it was all right. *Come on in. I'll serve you dinner, whoever you are.*

Behind her were the stairs, which separated night from day and man from woman, with Meg occupying the second-floor master bedroom and Jeff the ground-floor TV room. Danger in that division, too. And in the dining room, an implosive danger: the silent family gathered, as if bound, around the table. The father in the southernmost chair, acting caught, grounded. He'd almost gotten away but made the mortal mistake of coming back when called. The mother at north, waiting anxiously for everyone to grow up, wanting it and not wanting it at the same time. The daughter in the west testing her salted wings, seeing in the father her present fate (caught!) and in the mother, her future. And the boy . . . the boy . . . For the moment, the only danger Meg could see in him was that he was likely the reason the sheriff had introduced the word in the first place.

"Hey, Ben." Here was Jeff.

"Where've you been, Houdini?" Meg said. "I thought you were going to get the door."

"What's going on?"

"We have a little problem," the sheriff said.

"What is it?" Jeff brushed his thumb against his finger-tips. This struck Meg as the wrong gesture, one that implies lucre rather than the impatience she was sure he meant to convey.

"There's been a suspicious fire in the neighborhood," Ben said. "In the woods down the street from you."

"Fire?" Meg said. "It's so wet outside."

From the dining room table Katie could be heard saying, "It looks weird."

"It feels weird," he answered.

"He's shaved his head," Meg said, eager to divulge some news of her own.

"How bad?" Jeff said. "Anyone hurt?"

"No one's hurt. It didn't get very far."

"Why do you say 'suspicious,' Ben?" Jeff asked.

"I can't believe you didn't get in trouble." Katie again, at the table.

"I know," he said. "Me too."

"Clearly it was set," Ben said. "Probably kids. There was all kinds of activity down there, branches, an empty bottle of rubbing alcohol and other household solutions."

"Katie!" Jeff called.

"This doesn't sound like her at all," Meg said.

"You said yourself, Meg, she's a tough case."

"I didn't say that, Ben. I said she was tough. I didn't know she was a *case* at the time."

"Remember that one time—" The boy stopped himself. "Oh, never mind."

"What 'one time'?" Katie pressed. Was she testing him now, too?

"The fire, the fire," Jeff prompted.

"Whipped through the underbrush pretty good and got a few trees going," Ben said. "But it didn't get very far. Sandy happened to be driving by and radioed us. We got the VFD out right away, so we were able to nip it in the bud."

"They nipped it in the butt," Katie whispered, a hell of a whisper, loud enough to be heard at the front door.

The boy giggled, delighted, Meg knew, to be included in filial subversiveness. Meg waited for the coughing that always followed laughing.

"I thought I should get you guys on board," Ben said, "see if you've noticed anything unusual around here."

From the dining room table continued to come no coughing . . . and no coughing . . . and no coughing. You want unusual, Ben? *That's* unusual.

"Can you account for everyone's whereabouts today, help me retrace footsteps?" the sheriff said.

"You can touch it if you want," the boy said.

"Cool," Katie said. "Weird. It doesn't feel like a head. It feels kind of like a knee."

"That would be a really big knee." Highly risible, he snorted with more laughter.

"We just brought her home from school this morning," Meg said.

"Then we went right over to the hospital," Jeff said.

"The hospital?" Ben asked.

"Frank Ireland's office for a checkup," Meg said. "Asthma."

"Which he's outgrowing," Jeff added.

"Both kids have been with us all morning."

"More or less," Jeff said.

"Ben, what do you *really* want?" Meg said.

"I'm just asking some questions, gathering information. We have a lead. . . . Well, Joan Shearer says her boys saw your kids around those woods. And, well, your daughter's history of running away."

"That's a little extreme," Meg said. "Sometimes she wouldn't come when called for dinner. It's not like she took a knapsack and a Greyhound bus and we never heard from her again."

"Tron One and Tron Two," Katie said at the table. "With their chem-i-stry sets." Her falsetto note on *chemistry* cracked him up.

"Joan Shearer says—"

"Joan Shearer," Meg huffed. "And those ridiculous boys of hers. She's mad because I didn't invite her into my house. She told me those boys are glued to a chemistry set in the basement. How could they see anything from there? And with their Coke-bottle glasses, anyway. Bad eyesight all around, in that family."

"Meg, please," Jeff said.

"You should shave your head too," the boy said. "A bald girl! I'd love to see that."

Jeff could no longer contain himself. "Katie," he shouted. "Come here."

Laughter at the table turned to coughing. *Finally.*

Meg, too, could no longer contain herself. "Charlie," she called. "You, too."

Katie appeared in the doorway from the dining room. "Who? No one said 'Katherine.'"

"All the way over, please," Jeff said.

Her arms were welded across her chest, feet planted in defiance. Conscientiously objecting.

Jeff was sniffing the air again. Meg did not smell smoke upon her daughter's arrival—but she could see it. Katie's green eyes blazed and her skin was a lit red. Meg knew she could have started a fire in the woods as easily as she was standing there radiating fire right now.

"Do you have something to tell us?" Jeff said. "The sheriff is here for some very important business. Someone started a fire down by the dingle, and he has a report that it was you."

She shook her head.

"Are you telling us it wasn't you?" Jeff said.

"What if I am?"

"This isn't a game, Bear." Jeff's face blanched. "The *sheriff's* here."

"What's he going to do, arrest me?"

"No one's arresting anyone," Ben assured, more to Jeff than to Katie. "No one's blaming anyone."

"Yeah, right," Katie said. "Everyone's blaming me."

"We're just asking questions so we can find out the truth," Ben said. "That's all."

"She didn't do it," the boy said, joining them in the foyer. "*I* did."

He imitated Katie's stance, trying, Meg knew, to appear rebellious and angry, or at least inscrutable and teenaged. But his big, bald head betrayed the innocence of a baby, giving him away.

"I wanted to show her a goose," he said. "So we made— I mean *I* made—a fire so we maybe could scare it out. Then we'd have it."

"Yeah, then we'd have it," Katie said, following *his* lead, for a change.

"Can you tell me how you started it, son?"

"Matches," he said.

"And for accelerant?"

"Ben," Meg said. "He's not a criminal."

"I'm just trying to get some answers," Ben said. "Son, Charlie, can you tell us what you used to get the fire going? Besides matches."

"Air," he said, puffing out his cheeks and blowing long and hard, like he'd seen his mother and father do to the fire in the woodstove.

"Okay, thanks," Ben said, turning back to the adults, whom he wanted to come down to the sheriff's department. There was evidence they could take a look at, he said. All kinds of things to go over, and the house probably wasn't the best place. He invoked paperwork, procedure, protocol—music to Jeff's ears.

Yes, yes, yes, Jeff agreed. It made good sense to take care of certain things at the sheriff's office.

Meg's defense—"How can we leave the children at such a time?"—didn't even get off the ground. Ben had someone waiting in the car who could baby-sit.

"My, you're full of surprises, Ben," Meg said as he left the house.

Katie said, "Don't worry, Meg. *I'll* keep an eye on him for you." She draped her arm around him and ruffled his bald head. "Whoever he is."

•   •   •

Ben came back inside with his young niece, Lara Town-shend, who had been a student-teacher of Katie's at Union Valley Lower.

"Katie Carroll," Lara exclaimed. "When did you get so grown up?"

Lara sprinkled more magic dust over Katie by asking about her shoes. *Are they new let's see the heel where'd you get them . . .*

Katie, meanwhile, loved Lara's sweater. *Is it new let's see the back where'd you get it . . .*

Meg wondered what Lara Townshend was thinking behind this enthusiastic girl talk. What did she know? Meg had thought the rumors of *something's wrong at the Landry-Carrolls'* would begin as soon as Joan Shearer got home from the bus last night. But they had received no concerned, or even nosy, phone calls.

No one besides Joan Shearer had stopped by with a cake or a bread or a casserole. As for the scene on the bus, the neighbors (together or separately) could explain it away: Charlie Carroll had fallen asleep in his seat after a long ride, and his mother didn't want to wake him. That was why the bus lingered in front of the house until dark. Or the child had another asthma attack or missed his father. Perhaps he was angry, petulant, throwing a normal eight-year-old-boy tantrum and refusing to get off. No need to spread that around town, the daily struggle of mother and son.

Ben and Jeff went out to the cars while Meg went over a few things with Lara, momentarily breaking the spell over Katie by turning to the mundane: the list of numbers by the phone, what there was to help herself to in the refrigerator, the quirks of the woodstove with its high-grade dust-and-ash filter.

"You're not going away for a year, Mother," Katie said. "I doubt you're even going away for five minutes."

Meg caught her balance with a heavy step.

"Mrs. Carroll," Lara said. "Are you all right?"

Used to be she could leave the house for hours at a time. But the idea of leaving for *five minutes* now knocked the wind out of her.

"Should I get your husband?" Lara asked.

"He's not her husband," Katie said.

"I just need a little air," Meg said.

She stepped outside, and the girls followed, Lara with her arm around Katie. Jeff had pulled the car around front.

"What should we do with the house to ourselves?" Lara was saying. "Just us girls."

"Not just the girls," Meg said.

Where was he? She'd grown used to him underfoot.

"Charlie!" she called into the house. Loud enough for Katie to block her ears and Lara to actually hop back a step.

"Mother, he's not—"

"Charlie," Meg hollered over her. "Charlie Carroll, come here this minute!"

"He's not deaf," Katie said, "and neither are we. Well, maybe we are now." She hit the side of her head as if she had water in her ear from swimming.

A tap on Meg's shoulder.

"You rang?" he said.

She turned around. He squinted: *Who is she?* But he wiped that look off his face so fast Meg couldn't be sure it was ever there. Now that big smile and naked head.

She had made a pact with the sun and broken it. But the sun meant nothing to her. She hadn't yet made a pact with him. *If you are here when I get back, happy and healthy—and bald, I don't care—then I will never leave you again.*

"Wow, Charlie?" Lara said.

"Now introducing," Katie trilled, "my brother, Baldy. Baldy the Baby. Also known as Humpty the Dumpty."

He blushed and palmed his head.

"Nobody better have a great fall while we're away," Meg said, doing her best to recover.

"Puh-lease," Katie said, disgusted. "We're not children. Right, Charles?"

"We'll be careful," Lara said. "We won't let anyone break their crown. Oh, wait, that's Jack and Jill."

"What is it again that happens to Humpty Dumpty?" Meg goaded.

"He goes to live in a shoe," Katie said.

"No, he gets a little lamb," the boy said.

"Swallows a spider," Katie said.

Jeff raced the car engine, registering his state of readiness. He hated to wait and hated to diverge from his word. Ben had already left, and Jeff promised to follow right behind.

He came out of the car. "Let's go," he called.

"I'm just saying good-bye," Meg said.

"We'll be back in an hour."

"We were just trying to remember what happens to Humpty," the boy said.

"Dad will know," Katie said. It was hard to read her tone, whether she was making fun of Jeff, of herself for once having felt this way about Jeff, or whether she was actually, for a moment, feeling reverent.

"All the king's horses and all the king's men come to help," Jeff said. "Okay?" He tapped his foot dramatically, at once meaning his impatience and mocking it.

"Then what?" Meg said.

"Yeah, Dad," Katie said. "Then what?"

For her, the old Katie, Jeff pantomimed an arduous carpentry session, sawing, hammering, planing. "They try and they try and they try," he said, theatrically wiping a tired brow with his sleeve. "But they can't put Humpty together again."

On "Humpty," the boy touched his head again, in case anyone wanted to renew the connection to him. "Why would the king's horses try, I wonder?" he said. "Horses could never fix anything."

This brought a little levity, allowing the parents to head into town on a rising wave.

9

"WHAT IF THE SHERIFF'S Department comes to take him while we're away?" Meg asked on the drive.

A quartet of big raindrops fell on the car.

"I have no answer for that," Jeff said.

"How will we ever forgive ourselves?"

"I have no answers for these questions," he said, "because they're not questions. They're impossible riddles, and I don't know what you want from me."

Her thoughts snapped like elastic back to the house. Numbers by the phone could provide clues, had Lara been looking. Emergency, Pediatrician, Union Valley Lower and GMS, Helpful Neighbors—Palazzos, Ghearies, Cosgroves (not the Shearers, who were distinctly Not Helpful)—and, penciled in, Jeff in Toronto. Any of these numbers could fuel a spark of skepticism in Lara Townshend.

Helpful Neighbors were once friends, but distance, the internal pull of families, and the threat of dander and dust mites kept neighbors along these graded roads as what they were called in the detailed *Vermont Atlas*: "inhabited detached dwellings." Debbie and Vince Palazzo's house was as welcoming as they were, but was full of cats and dust, and, in the winter, a heavy smell of creosote. They had five kids, ranging in age from the baby to Donny, who was Katie's age and went to Union Valley Upper. Leah Gheary had five-year-old twins, rough-and-tumble Jack and Luke, whom Katie baby-sat for now and then when she was home, but whom Charlie seemed scared of. Greta and Thomas (long O) Cosgrove, a hearty couple in their seventies with an indistinct accent and a fiercely shedding Siberian husky, were always covered in dog hair, always walking, always waving hello and walking on.

Meantime, Union Valley Lower might ask why the boy had been absent so much. He should have been encouraged to go to school. A qualified school nurse on duty, a reliable emergency phone number, and a few doses of epinephrine on hand were all the mother needed to get a little time to herself. GMS might incite Lara to wonder with them why Katie was so reluctant to go home and be with her family. Meg hoped that Lara could satisfy herself with an obvious answer: because she was thirteen.

Pediatrician could tell Lara what he knew of Charlie Carroll, a young asthmatic whose prognosis rose and fell capriciously, driving his father away and his mother toward. And now, no explaining it, he seemed perfectly fine, like a whole new child.

Emergency, in the form of Ben Handke, could fill Lara in on the details of the case, which he must have put together by now. Why else summon them to the Sheriff's Department on the pretense of fire? Just ask the mother where she was the night before all this started, Ben would tell Lara. Ask her if she was *sure* her son was all right the other night, when she stepped outside to get some air, if she was *sure* he was sleeping the sleep of the dead.

"Jeff, doesn't it feel wrong—I don't know, dangerous— to leave him with a stranger?" Meg asked.

"She's the sheriff's niece, for Christsakes."

"Not 'dangerous' that way."

He could play any one of his usual games on the stairs and come tumbling down. He could experiment further with Jeff's razor. Anything in the house could turn into a weapon or a death trap. Or *Charlie* could come home—to find his mother gone and his sister with her arm around Humpty the Dumpty, singing *My baby brother sat on a wall, my baby brother had a great fall.*

"Oh, here it comes," Jeff said.

He meant the rain. Sporadic, smacking drops turned into a downpour.

"I'm sorry," he said. "I really have to drive now."

To prove his point, the car bucked a rut, then another. Meg braced the dash and the door, to steady the car from the inside. Jeff slowed down, and the car settled into this state of traction—not 100 percent, that was for sure, but somewhere in the 80 percent range.

Meg let go of the dash and the door. Tried to let go of everything. Give herself over to the rhythm of the rain, the swaying drive, Jeff riding the ruts as confidently as a surfer.

She would leach away her fears by picturing them, staring them down: the car slicing through mud (the image of hot knife through butter did come to mind), crashing into a tree or an oncoming heavy vehicle; the ambulance, also slip-sliding down the road, further jeopardizing the car, red-and-white flashing lights jazzy in a refracting rain. The children in dark formal clothes, Katie a new skirt and sweater, the boy a suit. Charlie nowhere to be seen. He must be with them, with his parents, on the other side of the grave.

All that Meg had done would get undone, beginning with what she had just gone over with Lara Townshend. The list next to the phone would come untacked, the refrigerator would be emptied, the woodstove's filter, almost as expensive as the stove itself, would be pulled out by the home's next occupants who wouldn't want to bother with its elaborate cleaning. Charlie's other asthma paraphernalia would get packed up, too, and donated to the hospital. For all the use they had these days, Meg probably could have packed them up herself a half hour ago, before she left the house for this, the last time.

The Landry-Carroll house would empty of Landries and Carrolls. Meg's sister, the last of the Landries, would come to take the children. Jeff's brother, the drifter-turned-capitalist now somewhere in Eastern Europe, certainly would not, nor would his icy, elderly parents, who did not like children in their house after dark. Holly had always loved the kids, especially Katie—whom she called her "would-be daughter"—even though she hardly ever saw them. This, taking care of orphaned children, *this* Holly would do. They had no one else.

Her father had had Meg. On Holly's rare visit weeks before his death, Meg had asked her—outright, for the first time—to stay, to help. Holly countered with rehearsal and concert dates that involved many other people and could not be broken. "It's not just me," she'd said. "It's a whole damn industry."

"I have an industry myself," Meg'd said. "Namely, a five-year-old child and another on the way. But I've been in this house every day for the last six months, making plans for him to die and for mother to shrivel up and blow away. While you're off doing exactly what you want."

"Exactly what I want?" Holly said. "How about exactly what *they* want? These six months"—she raised her hands to indicate the upstairs, where one parent lay sleeping and the other lay dying—"are what you're giving them. The last twenty years"—she fluttered her fingers along an imaginary keyboard—"is what I gave them. I think we're even."

When Meg came to, she was staring at a crack in the corner of the windshield, fascinated by how it split her vision. The rain had already dissipated into not much more than a mist. She pushed on the crack from the inside. Of course the glass was dry, and of course it did not come popping out. Windshields are required, by law, to hold flaws.

"How'd this get here?" she asked.

Jeff glanced over. "No idea. A pebble, maybe."

"How long has it been there?"

He shrugged.

"A week, a month, a year?" she said.

"Please," he said. "I'm driving."

"Make something up," she said. "Pretend you know. So I can hear your voice. So I know you're here."

"Know I'm here? I'm right—" He banged the fogged windshield.

"Yes, I see you're sitting there. I see you're very busy driving. But how about thinking? Feeling? What are you even thinking about?"

"You want to know what I'm thinking? I'm wondering why the doctor's file says you were unavailable the other night. When the QuicKonnect dispatcher called to follow up."

After she hit CANCEL, she was just going to step outside *for a minute*. There was nothing more she could do for him, sleeping like that. He was perfectly healthy. Or else it was too late. The sleep of the sound or the sleep of the dead. In the gloaming of the night-light, the two states were indistinguishable.

"The phone must have rung in Charlie's room and he didn't want to wake me up," she lied.

"You were asleep already? How long did they take to call you back?"

"This was what he did, Jeff. He always tried to protect me—especially from himself, from anything he thought *he* caused. For your information. He must have snatched up the phone so quickly I didn't even hear it."

Jeff struggled to see out of the windshield, which had gone opaque. "Goddamn defroster! Goddamn rain!" He rubbed with the heel of his hand, hard, as if he could rub right through glass, reach out and throttle the rain. "Goddamn it! God*damn* it!"

The defroster, fully cranked, was scared now. Nervously, it pumped tongues of solvent air up through the dash, lapping the windshield clear.

"That's better," Jeff said. "At least I can see the road again."

A moment too late.

Flushing of underbrush up ahead, a flash of movement, wrong and impending movement, followed by the agile mass of a deer. It leapt in front of the car, bounding twice, until it was a bull's-eye for the grille. Then it stopped. Deliberately. As if to warn them. Not knowing—with its terrible depth perception—that the warning should go the other way around.

Jeff bore down on the brakes and wrestled the steering wheel as the car swerved toward the deer's broad side. With the otherworldly clarity that precedes an accident, Meg could see right through the dappled hide—to the ruminating four-chambered stomach, the heart flooding with adrenaline, the horizontal rib cage bracing for the Saab's steel frame.

We could slide forever, we could stop right here.

Meg looked into the deer's reflective bright carpet of an eye, which showed not panic but a glint of the accident about to happen. Meditations tumbled out as time moved not forward but outward, like afternoon idyll. *We could panic, or we could turn into rocks of faith. . . . We could shout, or we could fall silent. . . . We could love this deer to make its death more bearable, or, for the same reason, we could forsake it.*

The crack of impact was instantaneous, but the instant stretched and stretched and stretched. Until it snapped. The deer was thrown a brief distance, about a car's length, but remained standing despite the obvious hole in its side. It quivered, shook like that goose outside the bus, and started running, seemingly in all directions at once, each leap its own disjointed journey, until finally, God knows how, it returned to the woods.

10

A BROWN-AND-YELLOW Sheriff's Department car was in front of the house again. Meg squeezed her door handle, hard enough to unlatch it. The car light went on.

"Wait," Jeff said. "Let me stop the car before you get out."

He did, and Meg ran across the yard as the boy materialized at the front door.

"What?" she called. "What's wrong?"

"Nothing."

When she got to the door, he moved his arms away from his body a little, as if to be carried, or at least hugged.

She remembered her pact to never leave him again, a pact that she knew, even as she formed it, was made to be broken. Of course he would be here when she got back, of course he would be happy and healthy and bald, and, yet, of course she would leave again. *Because* he was happy and healthy.

If only she could reach for him. *Hello!*

Instead she hugged her own arms, completing what she could of a connection, and hurried inside to the living room, where everyone else was lying on the floor, playing cards.

Lara jumped up. "You know Davis? He's just visiting us on a break." Her aggressive sunniness sounded defensive.

The Caledonia County Sheriff's Department car, it turned out, belonged to Davis Townshend, a sheriff's deputy and Lara's new husband.

"I was answering a call out this way, Mrs. Carroll," he said. "So I thought I'd stop by. For a quick hello."

"I told you you wouldn't be gone for five minutes," Katie said.

"Did you forget something?" Lara asked.

"We hit a deer," Meg said.

Lara gasped.

"Is everyone—" Davis started.

"Everyone's fine," Meg said. "Except the deer."

"Davis Townshend—the man with two last names." Jeff had come in the side door. He shook Davis's hand with both of his own.

"Mr. Carroll," Davis said. "Heard about the deer. I can give Animal Control a call, have them come and get the body."

"It's not a body," Meg said. "It ran off into the woods, minus the piece of rib cage it left in our grille."

Lara gasped again.

"Too much information," Katie said.

"It was hurt pretty bad," Jeff said to Davis. "I'm sure it went into the woods to die."

"How about the car?" Davis asked.

"Hopefully, *it* won't go off into the woods to die. I'll get it looked at over the weekend."

"Easter," Davis pointed out.

"Right," Jeff said. "Well, it is drivable. Bambi put a nice dent in the front-passenger side, but it's still drivable."

"We've been having a real deer problem this spring," Davis said.

"So I heard," Jeff said.

"Have you folks been having any problems?"

Meg interrupted. "Davis, what kind of call were you answering out here?"

"Tron One and Tron Two blew up their house," Katie said gleefully. The heat, so to speak, was off her for the moment.

"The Shearer boys were playing with a chemistry set in their basement," Davis explained. "I guess they made a bad mix. I'm told they've done this before. Their parents think they're science geniuses, so they let them do anything they want in that basement."

Of course. Of course it was the Shearer boys who had been playing with matches in the woods. Why had Ben come to the Landry-Carroll house at all? Because he knew the mother could not say, *Innocent! How dare you! I'm the mother, I should know!*, as Joan Shearer had surely said about her pyromaniacal boys.

"Anyhow, this time it turned out to be no big thing,"

Davis continued. "The younger boy has some first-degree burns on his hands—like you'd get from an iron or a hot stove—but other than that they're fine."

"No sir," Katie said. "They're not fine. They're geeks."

"Not now," Jeff scolded.

"They *are*."

"Katie, please." Jeff hyperextended his fingers. His manifest anger often began this way. "Let's not get started on anyone else."

"I have a question." Good boy, diverting attention for Katie's sake. "Do you think we could get a dog?"

"Oh, I'm afraid we'll have to wait and see on that one," Meg said.

"I would feed it and walk it. I would do everything it needed."

"First things first, as your father says," she said. "We'll have to see if the allergies in this house have run their course, for one thing."

"What if I'm asking Dad?" the boy said, puffing himself up.

"All right," Meg said, turning to Jeff. "What about it, King Solomon? What do you think we should do? Get him a dog, see if he's allergic?"

"I can't keep doing this, Meg," Jeff said, *sotto voce*.

"Does anyone want to know about burns?" the boy said. "Davis taught us. Does anyone know what kind of burns you get from an iron or a stove—like, what degree they are? I can tell you about burns, if anyone wants to know."

"You know what?" Jeff said. "*I* want to know." He turned

buoyant and jocular again, frighteningly so. "What is it about burns that's so damn interesting?"

The boy blushed all the way to his scalp. "What kind of thing do you want to know?" he said.

But Jeff's mind was already elsewhere. He was staring at the strewn cards on the floor, his attention consumed by them. Heat rose in Meg's face. *Jeff, look at him!*

"Do you want to know, maybe, what you're supposed to put on a burn and what you're not?" the boy tried.

Jeff was kneeling, gathering the cards. "Let me get these first," he said.

"How about you tell us everything you know," Meg said. "He's listening, even though it might not look like it."

"You're supposed to put ice." The boy was nervous, trying to make his voice loud and not loud at the same time. "You're not supposed to put butter or oil."

"Butter cooks 'em," Katie said. "Served with Tron One and Tron Two—grilled geeks." No one laughed, but no one yelled at her, either.

"Do you know why a sunburn turns red?" the boy said, addressing the top of Jeff's head.

"Jeff," Meg tried, for the boy's sake. "Jeff, listen."

"Repair work," the boy went on. "Cells have to do a lot of repairing. To the skin." He pantomimed carpentry, as Jeff had earlier, hammering in midair.

Everyone was watching him, everyone except Jeff, who was still gathering cards from the floor. The boy mimed sawing and planing and more hammering.

Jeff was doing a remarkably inept job picking up cards.

He lost so many with each sweep of his hand that he was making this an impossible task, one that required all his concentration.

The boy hammered, then pretended to drop the hammer, pick up something else and swing it like a bat.

Meg couldn't stand it anymore. She clapped her hands three times. She'd meant it as applause, as praise, but it sounded like discipline. The boy looked down, Jeff looked up, Katie looked away, and Lara and Davis shuffled awkwardly between themselves.

"You two," Meg said to Lara and Davis, "you're dismissed. We've changed our plans. We're sticking around for a while, so you're free to go." *All agents of the sheriff's department are free to go.*

"Are you sure?" Lara said.

"Ma'am?" Davis said, clearly uncertain of his official role here. Was he the sheriff's proxy, or was he a polite visitor in a troubled household?

"We'll be sure to call if anything explodes around here," Jeff said, jocular again, recovering his man-among-men disposition. He walked Davis and Lara outside.

As they stood talking by Davis's car and Katie disappeared into the TV room, Meg listened to the boy explain the rules of poker. Davis had just taught them how to play. Poker was very complicated. You can win money. There are lots of rules. You have to know them all or you might lose money. He was bursting with ascending values. *Two pairs, three of a kind, full house—that's two cards of one kind and three of another. It's hard to get.*

Davis was sitting in the open sheriff's car with his feet out as Jeff paced and gestured. *Cards in order but different suits is a straight.* If she blurred her focus, she could mesh her senses so it looked like Jeff was telling Davis the rules of poker. *Cards all of the same suit is a flair . . . no, wait, a flush.*

"Davis tried to teach us poker, but I already know how to play," Katie called from the TV room.

"Don't shout," Meg shouted. "Come in here if you have something to say." She looked down at the cards that Jeff had left, which were now a greater mess than before he started.

"I was just *reminding* you"—Katie stuck her head in the living room—"that Dad already taught me how to play poker. I was just being polite to Davis"—she took an exaggerated curtsy—"because I'm such a polite kid."

"Naturally," Meg said. "And maybe you want to help me pick up these cards." She knelt down and gathered them herself.

"I'm going outside, to see if anyone's home anywhere in this town."

"I should keep you inside when you're under suspicion of starting fires."

"*A* fire," Katie said. "Not *fires*, plural. Anyway, I'm sure it was the pyros next door. If you were a good mother, you would know that."

"If I were a good mother, I wouldn't let you out of my sight right now," she said, letting Katie out of her sight to pack up the rest of the cards. "If I were any kind of mother at all I would—"

"I think she left," the boy said.

Meg looked up at the empty doorway. "Just the two of us, then." She tried for some of Lara's aggressive sunniness. "So, tell me more about poker."

"Maybe he taught her how to play poker, but not me. I think he taught her lots of things that he didn't teach me."

"Parents teach different kids different things. Especially when it comes to boys and girls. There are certain things, I'm sure, that fathers teach only boys."

"Like how to shave?"

"Yes. Like how to shave."

That blush again. "Mom?"

"Mmmm?"

"Remember when I had hair?"

"You mean earlier today?"

"Yeah."

"Of course," she said. "Of course I remember."

"Um," he stammered, "do you think he likes me?"

"Who, Davis?"

He shook his head and looked outside as a car started up. "Jeff?"

He nodded.

"Oh, my," she said, breathing sharply. "Of course he does. We both do." She took a step toward him. Time had come for her to embrace him.

But he stopped her with a yelp—a sudden, urgent sound.

"What's the matter?" she said. "Are you hurt? Did you hurt yourself?"

He threw his head back and yelped again. He was barking. That was all. He left the house, barking and barking.

She watched him from the kitchen window. The mist and rain had cleared; late afternoon had flattened the light. His bald head was a beacon, begging her to keep it in sight at all times. How could she have thought that she could leave the house right now? The sheriff's department was a fine place for Jeff, but she should be here, keeping an eye on the children. Too late for Katie, who could not be contained, who was roaming the neighborhood right now, trying to find the Gheary kids, or pick a fight with the Shearers.

The beacon stopped at the edge of the backyard and began—what? barking again? Mouth wide open, cawing this time, it looked like from here.

When she got outside, she saw that he was trying to lure the goose, which was poking its head out from behind a tree. He was calling it like you'd call a dog. "Come here, come here," he coaxed, hitting his leg. The goose kept drawing its head back in that nervous way birds do, eyes fixed, bones so tiny that all movements are jerky. But it did not fly away.

He picked up a fallen branch and lurched at the bird. "Come here!" he shouted.

Finally it took off flapping.

He banged the stick against a tree for good measure, good riddance, until the stick splintered in half.

"Come here yourself," Meg called.

He turned around and pointed *me?* to his sternum.

"Well, I don't mean that goose."

He came over, arms folded across his chest like Katie.

"What were you doing over there?"

"I can't decide whether I like that goose or not."

"Either way," she said, "that's no reason to scare something. You should treat things—people *and* animals—how you would like to be treated."

"He hit a deer."

"Not on purpose."

"I wouldn't mind being scared, anyway, if I could fly. Like that goose or like Ray Gun Man."

"Well, you can't," she said. "So cut it out."

He was cradling one arm slinglike against his Vermont sweatshirt.

"What happened?" she said. "Did that goose do something to you? Did it bite you?"

"A goose wouldn't bite," he said. "It would peck."

"Excuse me, Dr. Dolittle. Did it peck you?"

"No," he said.

"Let me have a look."

He pushed up his frayed sweatshirt sleeve and turned his head away, as though she were about to administer a strong dose of medication—something a child, even one who had built up a tolerance, could not watch.

"Actually, Ray Gun Man can't really fly," he said. "People think he can, but what he really does is throws lasers and then walks on them. That's not the same thing." He prattled on, steeling himself for the arm examination.

Which was not coming. She could not bring herself to press and prod the fine arm of a healthy boy. She could not face holding a perfectly weighty and incarnadine forearm and saying, Does it hurt here? here? here?—all the while knowing that it doesn't, or if it does, it hurts only a little, just enough to remind mother and child that he's otherwise fine. She did not deserve this child.

"Okay, if you're sure it doesn't hurt," she said, across the gulf of not-touching.

He looked relieved, then puzzled. *Exam over?* "It hurt for one single solitary second when I was banging the tree," he said. "But it's okay now."

"That's what you get, then," she said. "A little sting in the arm. That's the consequence of scaring the daylights out of a defenseless animal."

"What's *consequence?*"

"The price you pay."

"Oh, yeah. I think I learned that word in school this year, or maybe last year. There's always so much to remember. Definitions, countries, times and divided-by, facts."

Another opportunity for Jeff's kind of test—they could quiz him against Union Valley's third-grade lesson plans. What Jeff didn't know, however, was that any breech in this boy's book learning could very well be Charlie's, he had been absent so much of the school year.

"Are you cold?" she said, eye on the threadbare sweat-shirt. "You're not dressed very warmly." The sun, after bat-tling rain on and off all afternoon, had dropped into the woods, leaving the two of them in shadow.

He summoned a shiver, unconvincing at first, a child doing what he's told. But then he seemed to *become* cold— as a feigned cough becomes an actual cough. A silhouetted bald figure, he trembled in the twilight chill, rubbing his chest as an old man might rub his tired heart.

11

"RAY GUN MAN?" Meg said.

"What?" Jeff said.

"That comic you used to draw for him—was it Ray Gun Man?"

"Which one is Ray Gun Man?"

"Honestly, Jeff, sometimes I can forget that you're the father."

"All of a sudden you don't know *me*?"

"Yes," she said. "All of a sudden."

Meg was in the bathtub, which was the only place to get warm thoroughly. Jeff did not seem to know where to go in this house anymore. He'd followed her upstairs after dinner, much as the boy had followed her around at first (him she had already sent to bed). Jeff had given himself a scotch as a prop, which he'd stationed on the hamper. It was the only coordinate that was truly his. He kept circling back to it, taking a sip, swirling the ice, leaving it for a moment so he would have something to go back to.

"Do you think we made a mistake not getting married?" Meg said. She was thoroughly warm now, and emboldened by it.

"Where on earth is that coming from?" Jeff said.

The bubbles had thinned out, but she did not feel naked. Her body looked swelled under the water, green-grayish, refracted. It seemed separate from her and well protected.

"Do you think things would be different if we were?" she said. "Do you think we've missed our chance?"

The shade swayed in front of the drafty bathroom window. The air was all frost and mud with the slightest hint of bloom. To Meg, in the bathtub, it smelled like weather coming in off the water.

"Our chance for what? Is this what's bothering you?"

"Do you miss him, Jeff?"

"Who?" He headed for his glass. "Please don't say Charlie."

"Charlie. Do you miss him?"

"Look, Meg. I don't know what I miss. Everything here seems like it was when I left. Except Charlie's better." He picked up his glass, sipping, swirling. "And I do think it's Charlie."

He sat on the shut toilet seat, setting his drink at his feet. "If you asked me again, that's what I would say. I wouldn't hesitate for a minute to call a spade a spade."

"Will you pick up your glass, please?" she asked. She had two rules for glasses, which she'd gotten from her mother: never put a glass on the floor, where someone's likely to kick it over; and never bring a glass into the bathroom, a high barefoot-traffic area.

Jeff balanced the drink on his knee, which was no better. "Go ahead," he said. "Go ahead, ask me again."

"You've already picked it up."

"'Is he Charlie?' Ask me that. Ask Ben, or Frank Ireland. Or Bear, for that matter. For Christsakes, you can even ask *him*. I think you know what the answer will be."

She wanted to join her body underwater, to be separate from herself, too, but she could not face the chill of resurfacing, wet-haired, to Jeff and his precarious drink.

"Will you leave the room so I can get out of the tub?" she said.

"Wait a minute," he said, standing suddenly, like an orator. "I know what you mean—Ray Gun Man. He walked on laser rays. But I never called it that, Ray Gun Man. I called the character Roger. That's how he talked, 'Roger *this*, Roger *that*.' The name was kind of a joke, I guess."

"Apparently he wanted a superhero more than a joke."

"I don't know anything anymore," Jeff said. "In this house, I don't know what to do when it comes to the kids. I call something Roger, my son calls it Ray Gun Man. You have no idea how strange I feel around here."

"We're all feeling rather strange around here these days," she said, "so how about chucking that excuse? And chucking me a towel."

Safely in her robe, she crossed the bedroom, catching herself in front of the full-length mirror. As with the deer, she could see right through the outer, the watch-plaid flannel, to a thickening in the waist and thighs. She now had haunches, salient enough to rival the breasts as the primary element of this female figure. She was surprised that she did not feel more burdened by physicality, given how much *body* she was.

Jeff stood behind her. A chill rose in her, as if that's what his presence did, released the cold.

"Stranger," he said. He covered her face with his free hand—more tenderly than a smother but shocking nonetheless.

"What are you doing?" she whispered into his palm, trying with her lips to find the flesh in it; it was thin and dry as paper.

Between his fingers, she could see the mythic figure of them—the faceless body of a woman with a man's head on its shoulder, an impossible combination that could exist only in legend.

She tried to find her eye in the mirror but saw no sign of it, no optic flash of cognition behind his hand. Without the particularity of a face, her body was not unlike the land up here: ample, archetypal, a primal example of form following function.

"I'm not sure where I am in all this," he said.

"Put your glass down," she said.

"You know what your body is to me?" he said.

"That's dangerous territory, Dr. Freud."

"A screen."

"Generous of you," she said. "If I knew you were thinking in that neighborhood, I would have said storm door."

When he walked away, she felt another chill, equal to the first.

He put his glass down on the far bureau. "I'm going to go get the car fixed tomorrow," he said.

"It's Easter weekend." She sat on the bed, peeled open the covers. Getting into bed—she could not remember when she had last done this—seemed better taken in stages.

"Silverman Saab will be able to take a look."

"So you'll be mobile again. That must be a big relief."

"I'm an inch away from the door, Meg," he said. "Don't tempt me."

"While you're there," she said, "will you turn off the light. I'm exhausted."

He turned off the light and closed the door, sealing himself inside the room, though still an inch from the door. He had a confession, he said into the night. When they first met, in Life Drawing class, he would turn the model into her. He'd arrange his desk so he would see her in the same line of vision as the model. "Every class," he said, "I would pretend I was drawing you naked."

This was not the confession. This, it turned out, was the flattery before the confession. Once they were sleeping together, he confessed, he hardly thought about her at all during Life Drawing. He saw the model only, line for line, as he would a building or a tree. He concentrated on the model's back, for instance, wondering why the spine, a load-bearing column, should lie so close to the surface that its bumpy outline is visible.

"One thing about you, Jeff. You don't know what to keep to yourself and what not to."

"Shouldn't I be able to tell you everything? After fifteen years."

"But you don't," she said. "Given that you hardly tell me anything, why do you tell me something like that?"

"He's getting *better*, Meg. We're all here, together. It's Easter weekend. I don't know. Maybe things don't have to be so hard right now."

On the wall, dark-on-dark shadows of trees formed a good exercise in line control and negative space. In the interlocking Vs of tree limbs, Meg saw this: with Katie, they came into relief as parents whenever she arrived on the scene. As it had been tonight, when she had come home by dinnertime but declared she wanted to eat in front of the TV. With her brother. Meg and Jeff agreed that that was all right for tonight, but only tonight. "Don't get in the habit of it," Jeff had said. Meg could easily have said the same. When it came to their fiery daughter, they would decide together on a course of discipline, whether that involved strict punishment or, lately, the more fearsome lack of it.

But with Charlie—and now with this boy—they were on their own, Meg and Jeff. They were parallel lines, able to preserve the space between them only by never meeting.

"Jeff," she said, "if you had to describe Charlie—say, to Ben, or to Frank Ireland—what would you say?"

"I don't know what I could have told them that you don't already know."

"I'm not asking because I don't know," she said. "I'm asking because I want to know what *you* think, how you remember our son."

"Okay, fine. Fine, okay? I remember when I left in January how he was sitting on the front steps. It was freezing outside, but he was just sitting there, all hangdog, holding a baseball glove. I guess it was his, but I don't know where it came from. I hadn't gotten him a glove yet. I was waiting for spring, or for him to show an interest. Whichever came first.

"Katie wasn't around," he continued. "She was still home, winter break, but she must have been at a friend's house."

"You, sir, got off easy. You should have heard what she said to me that night at dinner, which, by the way, no one ate. 'Are you happy now?' she said. That's what I got."

Sounds of mud season trickled into the bedroom: swollen backyard stream, dripping rain gutters, early spring river-moats running on either side of the road. Distant weeping somewhere in the march of April.

"What?" Jeff said. "What are you hearing?"

He opened the door. That let in no additional light or sound, did not expand the bounds of the room at all, which opening a door should do, even in the dark. He turned on the light. Too bright. He turned it right back off.

"Do you still hear something?"

"No," she said.

The light had burned a brief negative of Jeff into her vision, Jeff inside-out.

"Nothing to worry about, then," he said. "Any sound that disappears when you turn on the light is only a night sound. House settling, trees creaking. Something around here expanding with warmth or contracting with cold."

The guiding principles of mud season.

He joined her on the bed. "Maybe I should sleep here

tonight," he said, putting his hand on her leg. "It's been such a long time."

She drew away. "Not now," she said. "Not when you have this habit of disappearing."

"*I'm right here*," he said, clenching his patience, broken-necked, between his teeth.

"Okay, I have a confession, too," Meg said. She told him that one day she had left the house, just had to get out, leaving Charlie alone.

"When?"

"Years ago," she said.

And so, on the record, she went back to *years ago*. After driving the back roads came walking them. Stepping outside for a moment's respite from jangly crying, peppery coughing. Needing to stretch her legs. Stretching them on the front stoop, a little more in the yard, more still down the road.

"For how long?" Jeff asked.

"I don't know," she said. "Not long. Maybe a half hour. But that's not the point."

"Well, what happened when you got back?"

He was asleep, maybe, when she returned, or he was awake. Sometimes he was crying, sometimes not. But he was always *there*. No harm done, except for the seam that had been opened, the seam in time when anything could have happened.

"Nothing happened," Meg said. "The point is that I left him. I thought I was just stepping outside for a minute, for some air," she said, "but maybe I was trying to run away."

"You came back, though, and he was okay. Right? And this was years ago, right?"

"You don't have to forgive me so quickly."

"Maybe I want something in return." He waded his hand into the sea of bedspread between them, reaching for her at first, then, halfway, changing the gesture, turning his palm to the ceiling. Empty-handed. Or was it, Nothing up my sleeve?

She was too tired, too far away, too long ago to take his hand, along with whatever would follow, him spending the night in what was now her bed. She was too tired to finish the confession she'd started, to tell him that she'd left their son as recently as Wednesday night. Just the other night. As he lay sleeping.

When she first had her hand on the doorknob that night, she'd tried to keep herself inside by making a mental list, any mental list. So she inventoried the weatherstripping in the house, until he finally stilled to silent. Then she went back upstairs as though returning to a battlefield or a burgled house to survey the damage. Or going to check on her father, whose own condition could not be monitored audibly for the electronic bazaar in his bedroom. Television, radio, oscillating fan, player piano. But this house, her house, was so quiet.

The forces of wanting to see and not wanting to see were almost exactly equal, and she felt like she'd never get upstairs, each step smaller than the one before.

Increments *do* add up. Eventually she arrived at his doorway to find him lying peacefully on his right side, back to her. He was all right. Or all wrong. Either way, her PANIC did not circuit through QuicKonnect, which was lit up but which she immediately CANCELED. It circuited instead through her feet, then through the ground at the dingle, where she ended up. She passed the time alternately sitting on the rock and pacing the silty ground that felt like quicksand but must not have been, since it did, ultimately, release her. But not until the whole night had gone by.

She would not tell Jeff this. He would only forgive her. Forgiveness was his ticket out.

She did offer him a temporary pass, however, throwing a look of concern toward the door.

"Do you still hear something?" he said, popping up, ear to the dark. "This is an old house—a lot of movement. Structural, rodent. I'll check it out."

Jeff to the rescue. He would take to the house with a flashlight, track down noise until he had it by the scruff of the neck, its fists flying like a ragamuffin stowaway out of Dickens. Or would the sounds, any and all night sounds, disappear precisely because someone was after them? As with dandelion spores: the very act of reaching for them blows them right out of your reach.

She pinned her hopes on a mouse. *This time, please, let Jeff save the day.* Let Jeff find a mouse, flick it with a paper towel roll, cage it in a saucepan, somehow shuttle it outside, where it would only come in again but not tonight. Let him hold on to something. Let him perform a tangible act, for his sake anyway, if not the day's.

•   •   •

The gift of sleep came easily, but, like a Trojan Horse, it held an ambush. Dreams. Starting with her searching the house. Searching and searching but not touching anything, which made Meg-the-dreamer grow increasingly frustrated with Meg-in-the-dream. *Open the closet! Push the couch away from the wall, pick up the lid of the hamper. If you're going to look, look!* She finally realized she was searching for a baby. It was so small she despaired of ever finding it, but she knew it was around somewhere. *If only she'd put a little elbow grease into the looking.* She knew the baby she was looking for was hairless and genderless, with a pointy face and beady eyes. But she loved it. It was her baby. The dream was weighed down with a fear that she would crush the thing—sit on it, drop it, put a huge bag on top of it. That's why she wasn't touching anything, wasn't moving anything aside. As she searched, fear turned to dread, as she realized that she already *had* crushed it. She was looking for it for all the wrong reasons; she and the baby both knew that. *All the wrong reasons* appeared to Meg with the fleeting acuity of a dream, whose revelations always evaporate upon waking.

A muffled clatter from downstairs seeped up into her bed, at the edges of sleep. It was the couch in the TV room being pulled out. The noise refracted past, present, and future leave-taking like light through a prism.

Back in the center of sleep: yet another boy, this one older, long-legged, slouched on a couch, a dog on the floor next to him. The place seemed to be a small apartment. Late afternoon, late summer, to judge by the light—a particular change-of-season light that gave the boy's nut-brown hair a reddish cast.

She called him into a kitchen, where there was a cake with many candles, flames waving like faraway grasses in the wind, a blocky 13 in the middle. He pulled up a stool to the butcher-block island, and there they sat, two benign gargoyles whose human resemblance was striking. She was prepared to sing "Happy Birthday" as soon as he closed his eyes.

The dog shuffled into the room, nails clicking under sprouting gray footlocks. The boy slapped his thigh in too much encouragement, a gesture that seemed to mock the dog's labored trek across the linoleum.

For a moment, in the dream and in dreaming, Meg was heartened by the tableau: a boy and his dog. But something was naggingly wrong. If only he'd close his eyes, she'd sing to him. Why wasn't he closing his eyes? Why was he keeping her from singing?

He fluttered his long eyelashes toward the cake. *Should I go ahead?*

She nodded. He took a deep breath and blew out the candles. The dog shuddered a little with the exertion overhead. The room dimmed, minus the immediate flare of candles.

Coughing from down the hall. The first layer of waking, the shallowest, had her scrambling for the boy-in-the-dream, in a kitchen, thirteen, eating cake with a shaggy dog. Another layer of waking had her remembering her son was only eight. He was upstairs in his bedroom, and he needed her. They were the only two in the house.

Without passing through any more layers, she stumbled out of bed, navigating the dark by habit and by the fact that she was not alert enough for caution. Her hands guided her to the far wall, along the bureau which would lead to the door. *Edge . . . edge . . . edge . . .*

Until glass shattered and liquid splashed at her feet. She was so tired that she sank into soothing undersenses—the musical afternotes of broken glass, the vaporous waft of watered-down scotch—her half-sleep sealed rather than rent.

The suggestion of night-light beckoned from his open doorway.

Mummied in a comforter, pillow clamped over his head. Here he was, *buried,* and she had never said a proper good-bye.

She went to the foot of his bed, her exhaustion and the trailing scent of scotch about to work loose a confession, a plea for forgiveness, a good-bye to an entombed son.

But he kick-kick-kicked at her.

She pushed the comforter away. He was wrapped in candy-cane striping and steaming hot. He held fast to the pillow over his head, his fists two sturdy tent posts.

"Anyone home?" she whispered into the pillow.

She rubbed his back, larger and larger circles. Since when had he grown so much she could not span his breadth with one hand? *I barely recognize my own son*, thought the blind sensor of her hand.

"Charlie," she whispered. "Are you all right, hon? Should I stay? Should I leave you alone?"

She was dimly aware that she had sent his father away again, something that felt so recent and of the night that it may have been a dream.

The hillock of pillow shook its head, side to side, up and down, side to side. *No, yes, no.* She didn't know which response went with which question. Or if these were responses at all.

Her hand on his back gathered the heat and weight of a brand. She slid her fingers over to his ribs and began tickling a little life into him. He squirmed, laughing. Laughing and hiccuping, trying to hold on to his pillow while he wriggled. Laughing turned to coughing, and she stopped immediately.

"Okay, steady," she said. "We know how to go through this."

She tugged on the pillow, but he clamped down. "Remember the last time you had an encounter with a pillow?" she whispered. "We know how that turned out."

Muffled, it sounded like "No, how?" but it must have been "I know how." Charlie loved this story for some reason, and she'd been asked to tell it countless times, the story of the pillow, the feather, and the asthma diagnosis.

"You had just moved from a crib to a toddler bed," she said, settling into the familiar rhythm, "and you were taking a nap. Your mother was delighted, because she needed a nap, too. But you, sir, had other plans." She went on, telling how he started coughing and hiccuping, and couldn't stop. Nor could he say what was wrong. It turned out that he had inhaled a feather from his pillow, which kicked off a self-regenerating coughing fit.

He was still now, listening beneath his hypoallergenic pillow. He was so quiet, so blank. She jiggled his back. Nothing. Harder, shaking him now.

He threw the pillow off his head and sat up. "What?" he said.

"Never put something over your head like that," she said, in equal measures angry and relieved.

The pale blue night-light seemed to halo the hair right off his head. She reached to touch him, to dispel the shorn image, to feel the reassurance of her son's familiar curls, whorly cowlick in back.

The sensation, touching his bald head, read first as pain—shocking and wrong. And, as with pain, her immediate impulse was to draw away. But the next impulse, the struggling to make sense of her own senses, was something else entirely, shuttling along the synapses without purchase, without endpoint.

"What on earth—?" was all she could muster. She was shaking out her hand, trying to convert the feeling back into pain.

"Did you forget that I shaved my head?"

She shook her own head fiercely, which shook her fully awake. "What are you doing in those pajamas?" she snapped.

"Are they too hot for spring vacation?"

She let it go at that. Better he was wearing them than that they lay unoccupied on the floor, flat as paper.

"What about the rest of the story?" he said, bending toward her like a flower to light. *Tell me about me, tell me about me.*

This, she had to remind herself, was not a clue to his identity. Every child wants to hear stories about himself, whether he is who he is supposed to be or not.

She told the rest of the story in the third person: Charlie couldn't stop coughing, couldn't say what was wrong. In examining the bed, she saw the beginning of another feather poking out of the pillow case—as one drawn Kleenex begets the next. She rushed him to the hospital. Okay, only in the retelling did she rush him to the hospital. In actuality, she carried him on her hip until she found Katie in the backyard sandbox, packed the two kids in the car, and drove at the speed limit to the pediatrician's office. Dr. Ireland gave him Robitussin and two tall glasses of room-temperature water, and eventually he stopped coughing. But the exam revealed lasting wheezing, severe asthma, and a long course for the mother in caring for an asthmatic child, including trying to learn to give a shot by practicing jamming a needle into a grapefruit.

"Remember what the mother used to say after that?" she said.

Pricked by "remember," his glee drained visibly, like a blush goes down, or a water level. "Yes," he said.

"What?"

For a long while after that, whenever he broke into an attack she would stroke his back and say, *smooth the feather, smooth the feather*.

"It was a long time ago, right?" he said, tears grabbing at his voice. "I was only a baby, right?"

"You don't remember," she said.

He looked away.

Wait a minute. Thinking hard, she could feel herself making the phrase part of her breath—*smooth the feather, smooth the feather*—not saying it out loud after all.

12

THE PULLED-OUT BED—how it dominated the TV room—looked like an insult. Meg stripped the sheets and slapped the mattress fresh. This flat expanse struck her as the surface area of a common-law marriage laid bare, as you open your hand to show a begging dog, *See, nothing there.*

Did Jeff go straight back to Canada? Or would he stop first at the Sheriff's Department, to go on record, let Ben know what he thought? That this was indeed Charlie. He had thought at first that he couldn't say. If the mother couldn't say, how could he, the father, who had been away so much over the last year—how could he say? But now he had realized, of course he could.

She folded the bed back into a couch. Light of a new day shouldered in, but all it seemed to reveal was how dark the room truly was, hunter green walls, lots of cherry wood. Did Jeff feel closed in here, in this cul-de-sac of a room, or did he feel safe? Did such conditions even occur to Jeff?

She opened a cabinet to put away the bedding, pushing aside some old checkbooks and several packets of photographs. She couldn't help but look.

On top was his latest set of school pictures, two eight-by-tens, four five-by-sevens, and a Warhol grid of wallet photos, Charlie after Charlie after Charlie. School pictures were taken in November—a month that she remembered as particularly hard, heading into another winter, Jeff agreeing to a Toronto project beginning in January, Katie good and gone, Charlie doing battle with his "itchy lungs," as he called them—but he did not look troubled in these pictures. Even though they were all the same, she looked through them face by face, as if there might be a slight difference here or there, as if one might betray something the others hid. He looked, she would have to admit, generic against that cloudy faux-sky background. A cowlick, a gap between his teeth, a goofy smile. There was a washed-out brightness to his face that she did not remember him having. What was it about school pictures, she wondered—the thin, false light? nondescript setting? high-gloss finish?—that makes all children look essentially alike?

Then the orange-and-yellow Kodak envelopes. A summer vacation in Rockport when the children were little. This particular day had Charlie, pink from sun, wearing only a diaper, while Katie, tan as wood, wore a neon green bathing suit with a big blue flower at the hip. She was a little out of focus. She must have just arrived or was about to run off. Charlie, Meg remembered, was mesmerized by the ocean and could watch its changing edge for hours. Katie was alternately spooked by the ocean and mad at it. What bothered her most was that she had no control. Waves kept rolling in and out, even as she stomped her foot and yelled at them to stop.

There were pictures of Katie when she first started the local ski program, swaddled in fleece, yellow "Midas muffler" over her mouth, goggles over her eyes, hair tucked up into her helmet. No sign of Charlie. He was told he was too young to ski, and the issue was not revisited when he became old enough. At the end of the roll, a single picture of him playing T-ball. His one T-ball season. He had a pinch runner, although the doctor said he could try baserunning. Try it and see, Dr. Ireland always said. If it's a problem, stop, but don't rule things out before he has a chance. Meg envied the doctor, unburdened as he was by fear, love, guilt, exhaustion, need.

In another roll, Charlie and Katie were together (together! it looked so unlikely) in pictures of Union Valley Lower's annual Color Wars. That must have been two falls ago, when she was still in the lower school. She was all blue, in jeans and an old blue V-neck sweater that was too small on her and rode up her arms and belly. Charlie, meanwhile, was thick-cuffed in Katie's big yellow rain jacket. It was as if they had been photographed at two separate points in time: Katie in the future, once her clothes had grown too small; Charlie in the past, clothes waiting for him to grow into them.

There were also Charlie's pictures. She had gotten him his own camera in the fall, and he'd taken to the hobby. This roll was all shots of the lawn. Grass, some stones, more grass, a stick. Art? No, that stick was a garter snake. In each picture, he was trying to capture the disappearing garter snake, which might have been visible for all of a split second.

Under the photos was a pile of nursery school art, poorly preserved—glue humps on construction paper, with a few fossilized pasta shells and a dusting of sand and glitter on the shelf. She rustled the papers, swept sand and glitter into her hand.

Another packet of photos had been shoved to the back, this one white instead of bright orange and yellow like the others. These pictures had been developed differently, red digital date stamp from earlier this week. She hadn't seen them before. Charlie, marooned in the side yard, holding out his hand—as if he were showing something to the camera, but the camera was too far away for that, and he wasn't looking at it. Might have been a handful of seeds for the elusive goose. Meg had taken to keeping a small barrel of seeds in the garage so he could get the goose if he wanted, although it rarely worked. Often, nothing was lured by the seed. Other times, he would draw only what they called "regular birds," sparrows, robins, starlings.

She noticed herself in the border of this photo, standing in the side doorway. Just fragments, foot, sleeve, hand. Who had taken these?

Back to what looked like Charlie's point of view, askew, locus of interest unclear, off somewhere to the side. School, recess or gym. Knee-down shots of kickball, swatches of sky with a corner of jungle gym. Bright splotches of children, either too far away or too close up to make much sense out of. But there it was, in one children-far-off-to-the-left picture, that black, white, and gray argyle sweater. She couldn't glean much about the boy wearing it—dark haired, tall-seeming. A friend of Charlie's? Was *he* all right, the dark-haired boy who had parted with his sweater?

"Did he sleep here?" The sweater thief in the doorway, now in a plain blue polo shirt.

"What? Why do you ask?" she said, shoving the pictures back in the envelope, the envelope back into the cabinet.

"The bed was out."

"This?" She plunked down on the couch. Familiar impulse: cover-up. "No, it's not."

"It used to be," he said. "Just a second ago."

"Well, I don't know if he did. I was up all night with you."

"Me?" He looked surprised. "What was wrong with me?"

"Well, you're okay now," she said. "So forget it."

"What were those?" he asked, pointing to the cabinet she had closed so quickly.

"Just old pictures," she said.

He began backing away from her.

Away from *Who's this boy in the argyle sweater? Who took these photographs of you and me?* And away from the treasure trove of test questions she was sure Jeff had been looking for before he'd decided the answer for himself: *What's the name of this beach? What's the name of the T-ball coach? What do you call this, when kids dress up in different colors at school?*

"Nothing much," she said. "Don't worry. Just pictures of Rockport, Color Wars. T-ball with Coach Riley."

Even as she gave him all the answers, he continued to back away, right into the doorjamb.

"How tall do you think I am?" he said, standing ramrod straight, hand on top of his head. No, he was not frightened of her test questions. He was simply measuring himself against the door frame.

He turned to read his careful fingertip recording, which towered over the existing high-pencil mark.

Meg pinched the flesh between her eyebrows into a clover, pulling away the all-too-familiar question, *Who is he?* It had been years since she last measured the children against this door frame. All this proved, really, was that he was well taller than Charlie at five or six.

"Let me see," she said. She grabbed a pencil from the counter. "A person can't measure himself."

He happily squared himself against the frame again, trusting her, the mother, even as she downslanted the pencil to keep him from having grown, to keep them from having gotten to this moment.

He rubbed the pencil dent from his skull and turned around eagerly to see his measurement. But he couldn't find it. He kept looking where it *should* be, which was well above the false mark she had made.

As he searched, panicky, for his own height, Meg snuck out of the room. She headed to the living room, lured by a dawning need to check the woodstove. Bless farm families of the 1800s for building a maze of rooms, for a mother to get away if she had to.

The woodstove was still in early-morning ash. She was surprised Jeff hadn't tended to it. He must have been in a real hurry to get to town, to set the records straight, with Ben, with Frank Ireland. *Boy's fine, mother's the one to worry about.* He'd be driving fast—so much to do, to fix, to set straight. Speeding along, losing control, the Saab picking another fight with something in its path, maybe this time something its own size, steel to steel.

Footsteps closed in on the living room. She looped around to the mudroom, and when footsteps approached again, she grabbed a jacket and dashed outside.

She sensed the boy on the other side of the door, holding his tongue. Did he fear what she feared—that she was running away from him again? Had she told him the feather story last night not to share it but to give it away, a parting gift, a provision?

She tried to conjure a sense of mission, a sense of purpose to this desperate standing around. Jeff would have been able to summon purpose as soon as he stepped out of the house. If he had stayed long enough to stand in the side yard, his head would be filling with spring chores: rake the winter-matted lawn; clear broken branches from the edge of the woods; unclog rain gutters; tamp down the stream bed against runoff.

The sun was peeking out, and the smell of rain lifted off the grass. Meg realized she had grabbed Sandy's windbreaker, its ill fit creating a draft. She put her hands in the pockets and wrapped the jacket across her until she felt bandaged.

Out of nowhere, the goose flap-landed in the yard and started walking a jerky circle. She could see where "pigeon-toed" came from. And "bird-brained." Why wasn't it afraid of human presence? It could have alighted anywhere, yet it chose a spot not six feet from the only visible human.

Up close, the barrel-chested thing was a dirty sponge of a bird with its brown-on-brown feathers. The beak was outlined in kohl. And the honk had a scratchiness to it, as if the long throat were filled with grit.

The boy had snuck outside behind her. He did not want to bother her, she knew, but neither could he pass up an opportunity to be with the goose.

"There might be seeds in the garage," she offered.

"That's okay. I'm just looking."

The goose lifted off and flew a low trajectory into the woods.

"Remember when I was little?" he asked. "You used to say all the time, 'You're a goose. A silly goose.' Remember that?"

She did not remember. It was something she could have said. It was something *any* mother could have said. But she did not remember. Her eyes blurred with tears. Adrenaline, the blessing and the curse of a very advanced nervous system, shot through her. She ran across the yard to the road.

Mercifully, the school bus came into view right then and became what she was running toward. She would finally give Sandy back his jacket.

13

"IS THIS OKAY?" Sandy asked as he accordioned the door closed behind her.

"Yes, fine," she said, although she was not sure what he meant.

The aisle was narrower than she remembered, and the backseat not so very far away. What had felt like an auditorium before now felt every bit like a school bus. If only she had converted her first impulse—*right now, young man*—into actual discipline. Maybe she should have threatened him with consequence, vowing to ground him or send him to his room without supper. Or, a more appropriate punishment for Charlie: send him to his room *with* supper, make him eat. She was the mother. She should have been able to get her son off the bus in an orderly, unremarkable way.

She stared at the empty backseat, the one on the left, where he had been sitting. How had such a thing happened? Suddenly, in a cloud? *Poof*, a new boy? Or gradually, cell by cell, with time passing differently on the bus than in the outside world? Or had there been another redheaded boy who had noticed Charlie—redheads always catch one another's attention—on the bus, at school, in town? Maybe it was a prank, or maybe the boy wanted to escape from his life.

Between the two backseats was the EMERGENCY EXIT, unabashedly labeled, like the PANIC BUTTON. She was grateful that at least sometimes these possibilities were spelled out.

Sandy was busy adjusting his seat, the steering wheel, and the side mirror, as if he had just taken over the job from a different-sized driver. He fiddled with the rearview mirror, big as an airplane wing. He couldn't seem to take his eye off it.

She willed him to drive. *Get us away from here.*

Then she saw what he must have seen in the mirror— the boy, running toward the bus.

"Sandy," she said. "Go."

He put the bus in gear.

Relieved, she watched the boy in the mirror as they pulled away. She had to remind herself that he was growing smaller and smaller because he was getting farther away, a trick of perspective, not because he was shrinking.

"I think it'd be better if you sat down," Sandy said as he upshifted. "For safety's sake, I guess. For my sake. So I know where you are."

She took the front seat, behind the driver's. Poor boy— probably thought he was hitting a growth spurt until, twenty minutes ago, she cheated him out of inches, and now perspective was cheating him out of the rest.

"I'm going to Cherryvale to get the snow tires off," Sandy said. "In case you're wondering what I'm doing driving by your house on a Saturday morning. We usually take the busses in on the first Saturday of spring vacation."

She hadn't thought to wonder. It had seemed perfectly logical to her: he was driving by her house on Saturday morning to pick her up and take her away.

"What was that about?" he asked, tapping the rearview. "What do you think he wanted?"

"Too much," she said. "Whatever it was, it was too much."

"It looked like he wanted to show you that goose. He was pointing off somewhere and kind of flapping his arms."

"I've seen it half a hundred times. And I could stand to get away. Thank you for stopping. And thank you for going."

She was struck by how burdened the bus acted, straining and creaking along the corrugated dirt road, which was in need of regrading. The bus's protests must have gone unnoticed when it was full of children. But Charlie was the last one off. He would have had plenty of time alone on the bus to feel its reluctance.

How did such a lumbering thing ever get anywhere? Jeff had gone into town no doubt to turn her in, and here she was in a huffing-and-puffing getaway bus. Even with its body damage, the Saab could easily catch them.

"How are things with your husband?" Sandy said, trying, but failing, to sound indifferent, businesslike. "How is it to have him back home?"

"He's not my husband. And he's not back home," she said. "He's here, but he's certainly not back home."

She pressed her foot onto the floor, as if she had a gas pedal. "Can we talk about something else?"

"Sure, what?"

"Anything. Anything else."

"Okay." He began to narrate his route. After Charlie came the Shearer boys, who perched themselves right up in the front seat and talked about their experiments and how they were probably the smartest kids in the school, at least in science. Then the Gheary twins, followed by all the Palazzos. At the fork, Sandy picked up the loner Meghan Tarr, little Davey McGuinness, and Brandon and Camus DuBois with their polite Canadian accents. When the road turned paved, the Barnett triplets clamored onto the bus with their sad-sack older sister, whose light seemed permanently dimmed by the shining trio, three marvelously towheaded freaks of nature stuffed into the small Barnett house, which did not even have a foundation, he happened to know. At the junction of the County Road and School Street, a stop that the kids had dubbed "Max Corner," came Max Potter, Max Lamb, and Maxie de la Peña.

All this reminded Meg of the mock brain teaser: *You're the bus driver. At stop #1, ten people get on. Stop #2, four people get on, three get off.* And so on, to the trick final question: *What color is the bus driver's hair?* Blond turning silver, in Sandy's case. Lovely. Catching glints from the fickle sun.

At the stops nearest to school, he continued, many kids opted to walk in the nicer weather. He would pass them weaving like little drunks on the sidewalk, lopsided by their big backpacks (what did kids have to carry, anyway?), jackets flapping against them or dragging behind.

He could show her the route, he said. He would get to Hunger Hill, where there was a wide gravel expanse for him to turn around, then they could double back, head to the school if she wanted. No sooner had he said this than he drove right past the turnout. He looked wistfully into the rearview mirror and apologized in the manner of a leader who's lost his way. That's the only place to turn around for a while, he said. The road's so narrow. Sometimes he was surprised, he said, that the bus fit down this road at all. In agreement, branches slapped the bus like the plastic tentacles of an automatic car wash.

"If this mud gets any worse," he said, "some of these roads won't be passable in this two-ton thing. At least winter's almost over. All downhill from here."

Just then, the road turned uphill.

After a silent while he said, "I don't normally pick up hitchhikers, you know."

"And I usually don't get onto school busses that have been staking out my house," she replied.

Abashedness rose in his neck.

"Better yet," she said, "let's not talk at all, just drive."

Sandy nodded, playing by the new rules already. He shifted in his seat, fiddled with the gearshift, replanted his hands on the wheel. Gearing up for the long haul, it looked like.

She pictured the Saab, meanwhile, with a new, slightly different-colored front passenger side, coming to spirit the kids up to Canada, in a legal extradition and a promise of a better life.

She could run back to the house faster than the bus could get her there. Sandy couldn't even find a spot to turn around.

"Stop the bus," Meg said, as sharply as she had said *Go*.

He stopped. He lowered his head in apology. He tilted the rearview mirror toward the floor. Everyone, everything, was sorry.

He didn't dare look up when she got off, knocking by his arm for the door lever.

She understood why that deer had moved as it had. Fielding conflicting signals from the mind and the body, the feet *can* seem to travel in all directions at once. She darted in a sequence of broken lines, from tree to tree. She kept brushing against drooping branches, dangling leaves (from another season; it was too early for this season's leaves). The woods felt like a crowd. She felt an empathic cramp in her side. *Thump.* Right below the rib cage.

As soon as she could no longer see the road, she lost all sense of direction. Any given field—these birches, that rock, this crisscross of roots—seemed repeated over and over. Like a van Gogh. His wheat fields with no center, wavy patchworks creeping up to the edge of sanity. You could not tell which way was out.

She recalled the précis of a Figurative Landscape class: everything is a landscape. A still life is a landscape of domesticity. A portrait, a landscape of features, of the body. An abstract, a landscape of consciousness.

She caught her hand on a particularly unforgiving branch and twisted her wrist. The pain invigorated her, gave her something to focus on, transported her to the present. To the woods, to the rustle of leaves, creaking of trees, a rising symphony. The whole place was alive. A small animal with a big tail skittered through brush. A pheasant bustled by. She kicked at the ground, at the mat of pine needles and leaves, and the pheasant hustled away.

"Meg . . . Meg Landry . . ." Sandy's distant voice seemed to come from every direction.

Overkill. Or overestimation. He no longer needed to surround her like this, from all directions, in order to get her away from her family, or her family away from her. He probably hadn't even needed to bring home the wrong boy on his school bus. It might have been enough to lure her out of the house in Jeff's absence, to that changing patch of ground outside the bus, snow and ice and mud, no trace of footprints.

The woods were littered with patches of old corn snow. Could she be tracked here? Could Sandy? This ball-bearing snow could barely hold a foot, let alone a footprint. Its days were numbered, anyway. Winter was over. Its tracks would vanish with spring, as they did each year. Maybe that's why the deer had loped off into the woods, to cover death's tracks with those of changing season.

The other day, or week, or month (she could locate it in time only as *before*), Charlie had reminded her that when he was little he used to try to save this endangered spring snow. She had not remembered, but he kept prompting her. He had collected handfuls from the edge of the woods, the edge of the house—*remember?*—and put snowballs in the freezer. He had been about five then. She had wanted to cover them with Saran Wrap since they were studded with dirt, gravel, and leaf bits, but he had protested. *Remember, Mom?*

And then, slowly, she had remembered. "That's right," she'd recalled. "You were afraid the snowballs would suffocate."

The details had come back to her. She'd remembered the anxiety in his five-year-old voice as he told her how he had learned in school that oxygen is what you breathe, that there is oxygen in water, and that snow is water. She'd remembered that she had tried to untangle these truths in order to show the truth at hand—snow cannot suffocate—but she found in the end that it was easier to pile unwrapped snowballs in one corner of the freezer.

This would be a good test for the new boy in her house. "Can snow suffocate?" She could picture him patiently explaining how snow could not suffocate, how only people or animals, things that are alive, could suffocate. Maybe a plant could—plants are alive, too—but he wasn't sure.

Remember when you were five? she could ask. *Tell me about it. Prove it.*

"Meg . . ." Sandy's voice was getting closer, bearing down, pressing in.

So were the ambient noises, hum of birds and wind and insects. She thought of her father's sickroom, droning and whirring and crackling, as he may—or may not—have tried to call out her name. He could barely speak, she could barely hear.

Red, something red, flashed in her peripheral vision, near a trio of conjoined birches. The sun could no longer fool her with its trick of russet light—the boy has no hair! She knew it was only leaves, a bird, something that happened to catch auburn's wavelength on the visible spectrum of light.

It was impossible to run, really run, through this maze of trees, rocks, and roots. She had to stop every few steps and close her eyes, find her equilibrium, hold on to whatever was near. The energy she expended equaled the frustration of not getting far. She was working against the very curve of the earth.

When heavy breathing finally caught up with her, she thought for an instant that it *was* the snow, that snow could indeed suffocate.

"Pretty tough going, huh?" The gasping was, of course, coming from Sandy Tadaveski, who was standing in front of her holding his side, fresh out of breath, as benign as ever.

She was relieved to see him. Maybe she had been running not to get away but to be searched for.

"I . . . I had to get out of there," she said. Her breath was stitchy, too.

"I can see that," he said.

"That bus," she said. "How can you stand to be on that bus?"

He took a step closer, bent still nearer. The more he leaned toward her, the surer she was that he would go away, the angle of reflection equal, as it is, to the angle of incidence.

"I can walk from here," she said abruptly.

"Sure," he said. "But you're heading the wrong way."

He held her shoulders, as though *toward him* was the right way.

In the name of orientation, she held onto him. They sank to the ground, the spinning earth more manageable from there.

She felt a sudden drop in temperature, as though she had taken a plunge. Nothing mattered out here—that's what she loved about the woods. They were so vast they could absorb whatever happened, atoms of occurrence dispersing with light and air.

The bus was on its way back to the house. Meg was sitting in a middle row. She didn't want to be too close to Sandy, but neither did she want to be too near the EMERGENCY EXIT. Until he found another turnaround, she had been letting herself believe that Sandy was going to keep driving in the wrong direction into the next town, the next county, the next state. Maybe there was an underground network for adults, too.

The sun blinked out from behind clouds. At the same

time, it started raining again. This is how the days will go from now on, she thought.

"Have you ever been married?" she said. Softly. Softer than a regular speaking voice. He could not hear her up front. She let the question go for a moment then asked again, louder.

"No-o," Sandy said, questioning more than answering.

After a considering silence, he told her that he did have a child. A ten-year-old son with cerebral palsy. He had seen the boy only once, since the child lived in Michigan with his mother, a woman with whom Sandy was briefly involved. Sandy had seen him when the boy was less than a year old, but he thought of him often and could picture him as a ten-year-old.

"I had no idea, Sandy."

If she were a school child, she could throw something up the aisle at him—an eraser, a crumpled-up piece of paper—to further a budding crush.

"Of course, I could be picturing him all wrong," Sandy said. "Maybe he doesn't look as much like me as I think."

A serious rain pummeled the bus, hard enough for Sandy to stop driving. They were about a quarter mile from the house.

"Nature changing the subject," he said. "Enough about me . . ."

Despite sheeting rain, the sun lanced through clouds, making her squint.

It was a beautiful sight, the metallic, rain-dappled light of a sun shower—everything at once, a fireworks finale.

"Boy, I never talk about myself like that." He stood,

implying that all that talk about himself made him need to stretch his legs, to walk as far as the middle row.

"There's something I want to tell you," he said.

He was standing right beside her, but they would not meet each other's eye. All glimpses and senses. Sandy had none of Jeff's brooding remoteness. Jeff's deep green eyes took in everything, betrayed nothing. Katie's, too. Sandy looked more familiar than he should have, given how little she knew him. Meg wished she *were* a school child, wished she *could* throw a pencil at him and, simple as that, change the pledge of her affection.

"I really do like your place," he said.

There were times when she came home, either in the car or on foot, and could not imagine herself on the inside of the house she was looking at. The door looked like a foil, a trap, a barrier to passage rather than a conduit. She suspected there was a secret entry somewhere out of sight—in the same place, she supposed, as the secret exit, where, one by one, everybody had been filing out.

"Not only the house," Sandy said, "but the whole setup, the big yard, the woods, the outbuilding. Everything."

"That's mostly Jeff," she said. "The house was a swayback shell of a thing when we bought it, and that outbuilding was practically rotted away. He did an awful lot of work." She wondered if Sandy could hear her nerves thrumming against her voice. "He said he always wanted a barn. Though he turned it into a painting studio for me. For me to hardly ever use, is more like it."

"There's more to it than the house," Sandy said.

She tried to remember what more there was to it than the house. A father: feeling like a stranger with his own children, he becomes one. A daughter: sensing that leaving is a privilege afforded only to the strong, she becomes strong enough to go away herself, so she is not the last one left, holding the bag of family. A son: whoever he is, he is the only one who seems to be trying anymore. In fact, he's blurry with trying, inexact with it. The mother: she suddenly feels like poor God on the seventh day, bereft of and betrayed by what she's wrought.

"That's why I . . . well, I don't know what came over me," he said, "but when Charlie left his camera on the bus the other day, I snapped a few pictures with it. Thought you wouldn't mind having some pictures of him out in the yard. I half thought I might catch you, too, coming outside."

"So, you took those?" Already, the photographs loomed as memories to Meg, images of her and Charlie distanced by time and circumstance rather than by actual distance and an optical port. And now, further distanced by Sandy, mystery solved.

"When I saw I'd finished the roll, I thought I'd go ahead and get it developed for him while I was in town, give him the photos and camera back on the bus the next day. He seemed a little embarrassed. You know what he said?"

"What?"

"Asked me if I wanted to marry his mother."

"What did you say?"

"I said she's already married."

"No," she said.

"Good as," he said.

He put a knee down on her seat, boxing her in. She eyed the EMERGENCY EXIT over his shoulder. He leaned in further until they were kissing again. She braced one hand behind her and reached for his collar with the other. He smelled as common as soap. She hadn't noticed out in the woods, with so much else vying for her senses. His hair was so fine that it kept disappearing to her touch. She concentrated on him, *Sandy in particular*. Sandy was the one—savior or judge—who had delivered the new boy to her. Sandy was the one whose face, the last thing she saw before shutting her eyes, was looming in silhouette behind her closed lids.

His breathing, anticipatory, sounded like approach. Hers sounded like hammering.

Unless it *was* hammering. Unless Jeff had come home and was working busily and angrily in his woodshop or out by the barn, hammering it shut since she hardly ever used it. Or hammering the house shut. That would teach her to leave.

Meg pulled away from the bus driver.

"What?" Sandy said, wincing at the interruption.

The hand she'd been bracing behind her must have absently been trolling the seat's crease. She plucked something chunky and palm-sized. A transformer? A fat Magic Marker? An inhaler.

Had Charlie been on the bus again—yesterday, today? Ditched another inhaler? Had Sandy known where he was all along?

"What do you have there?" Sandy said.

She held up the inhaler, chagrined. She couldn't keep track of the most basic safety precaution for an asthmatic child. Couldn't keep track of the *child*, for that matter.

"From your jacket pocket," he pointed out. "*My* pocket, technically." He patted the windbreaker, letting his hand linger at her waist.

He was right. The plastic had a trace of the pocket's mint and wood smell.

"So," she said, "you said you had something to tell me?"

"This," he said. He moved his hand to her cheek. "Isn't *this* something enough for you?"

She shut her eyes. When she opened them, he was still there.

"I have something to tell you, too," she said. She looked at him long enough to notice that one of his brook-colored eyes was smaller than the other. "My father died—" she started.

"Oh, I'm sorry—"

She shook her head. "Almost nine years ago. Right before Charlie was born. He had lung cancer, an awful thing. I practically lived with my parents during those last six months or so. My mother was—still is—incapacitated by depression. I had my own family then. Katie, Charlie on the way, Jeff starting a practice. But I spent all my time with my parents, my father."

"Of course."

"But I wasn't there when he died. I had spent all that time preparing for him to die, waiting for it, then I wasn't in the room when he actually did."

"I'm sure that doesn't matter," Sandy said.

"I was right there in the house, doing something, anything, nothing. I never did anything of consequence in that house except wait. But he had all this noise going in his room, the television, radio, even a little player piano they had carried in their store years ago. So I couldn't hear anything."

Sandy sat down across the aisle. "Maybe he *wanted* to be alone."

"He was getting better, Charlie was," she said. She saw why Jeff and Frank Ireland kept saying this. It got the future in motion.

"That's what you want, right? You don't sound very happy about it."

"You sound like Jeff."

He stood up, looked like he was going to walk away. "That you can probably keep to yourself," he said.

Something caught his attention out the window. "Hey," he called.

Outside the bus, the kids were watching. How long had they been there?

"Katie," Meg yelled.

In black jeans and a sweater darkened army-green by rain, Katie looked like a camouflaged little soldier as she ducked behind a tree. The boy remained in plain sight.

Meg hurried off the bus, calling, "Wait right there."

Sandy echoed, "Wait," whether to her or the children she didn't know.

They took a few getaway steps up the road before stopping.

"Come back here right now," Meg called. "Both of you."

The boy was torn, she could tell, between pleasing her and keeping slow, begrudging step with Katie.

"Pronto, please."

Lucky for him the road was as muddy as marsh. He could look like he was trying to hurry, to please the mother, while actually lagging with Katie.

"What were you doing?" Meg asked.

"Nothing?" he said, raising his voice and, with it, her suspicion.

"*Nothing.*" Katie corrected his tone; it should have been disgusted rather than apologetic. "There's never anything to do around here. Can't even start a fire—it's way too wet." She began to walk away. "If that's what you, or anybody else, was thinking."

"Katie!"

She wheeled around. "What?"

"Wait for us. That's all. Just wait for us."

"You walk home with him," Katie said. "He's *yours.*" She broke into a jog.

The two of them, alone again. They were each keeping the other's pace, as intrigued strangers will do. He snuck sidelong glances at her until she noticed what he must have wanted her to: they were walking in parallel tire tracks. He seemed delighted by this. There were all kinds of jags in the track, where the bus had slid in the mud. She could hear the motor still idling behind them. Sandy, as usual, would wait for her to get home.

It had stopped raining again, and clouds seemed to be

rolling away in earnest. In spring, sun brought heat. In winter, a cloudless sky meant a cold, bald day. In the borderland of April, would this clearing warm the day or cool it?

"Want to name some rocks again?" she said after a while.

"Sure." He scanned the road.

"Mica," he said. "It looks like a mirror."

He picked up a stone and brushed it off. "That's not mica," he said. "I thought it might be, underneath, but it's just a regular gray rock."

"Samsonite?" she asked.

"There's no such rock," he said. "At least as far as I know."

"What were you really doing in the woods?"

"Nothing?" he tried again.

She fixed him with a look. He took a deep breath and puffed out his cheeks. Poor thing—holding his breath was all he could think to do to keep a secret. "I can't tell you," he blurted. "I promised I wouldn't tell."

"I don't care what you promised," she said. "I'm the mother."

"We were spying on you," he confessed.

"What did you see?" She wiped her lips, hard, with the heel of her hand.

"Mr. Tadaveski going like this." He stuffed his hands in his pockets and rocked a little.

"That's all?" she said.

"And you going like this." He moved his mouth rapidly, as if in a silent movie, to imitate someone talking and talking, someone who thinks she has finally found the right person to confess to.

"What else?" she snapped. "How long were you there?"

"Nothing. For a second, really. We were really just playing with that damn goose."

"Don't talk like her. One teenage mouth is enough for one house, thank you. Now, as for spying, that's a very bad idea."

"It was her idea."

"I believe it," Meg said. "But still. Spying is not only impolite—it's dangerous. You could find out things you shouldn't know. There's no way to give something back after you hear it."

"Okay." But he was distracted, his attention having shifted to the stone in his hand. Several times he lowered his palm to drop it but didn't. Here was something he had cleaned and cared for, even if it was only a stone. He seemed unable to return it to the muddy road. Finally, he put it in his pocket.

"Ummm, can I show you something?" he said. He bowed his head like a horse preparing to nuzzle.

He is still shy of me, she thought.

Then she realized, no, he was showing her his hair. Stubble was coming in already. Darker, it would now require a certain cast of light and wishful thinking to be seen as red. He leaned toward her expectantly, heliotropic as usual.

What does he want from me?

Nothing came his way—no touch, no punishment. Adding insult to injury, a wind kicked up, its suddenness (more than its strength) knocking him off-balance. He thrust out his arms. A square of paper fell from his jacket pocket and landed in front of Meg. She picked it up. A soggy photograph of Charlie standing against the side of the house. The red digital date readout was jarring, incongruously exact for such a faraway picture. Even from this distance, though, she could make out the wary stance, as if he were facing a firing squad.

A similar look here and now, as he jammed his hands in his windbreaker pockets. "That's a picture of Charlie," he said.

"I can see that," she said. "Do you want it back?"

He lowered his head again, and she returned the picture, which he put back in his pocket. He started taking his steps with exaggerated caution.

"What are you doing?" she said.

"Step out of the track, break your mother's back."

"Be careful, then," she said. "And thanks for the warning."

14

SANDY CROSSED THE LAWN, carrying something limp and bloody in his outstretched arms.

Meg hurried outside until they faced each other like duelers, several paces apart.

"What, Sandy? What is it?" Sandy Tadaveski, the bearer of her family's bad news.

"Your goose," he said.

Her eye tried to configure the raw thing back into a goose, although the meaty smell in the air told her she shouldn't try to visualize it intact or alive.

"Sandy, my God. Drop it."

He laid the bird in a heap on the grass. Meg approached as if entering cold water, by small, acclimating steps, until she could stand to look at it. The long, dirty neck was broken into a zigzag. She made herself look at the head. Flesh and feathers, loosed from the skull, were souped in blood. The pulpy mess was flecked with bits of color, like confetti.

Oh, she hoped for the boy's sake that they had not been seeing the same goose all the time. She hoped that there was more than one on the property, that another would poke its rude head out from behind a tree before he even noticed a goose was missing. Surely, she assured herself, where there was one goose there was a flock, or at least the mate-for-life. It seemed like the same goose all the time only because the human eye is anthropocentric, does not register the nuances of another species.

"What happened?" she said.

"Found it at the edge of the woods," Sandy said. "It was attacked."

"What on earth are you bringing it here for?"

"I have a hunch," he said.

"All these catamounts, deer getting more desperate for food . . . What does this have to do with us?"

"I think you know," he said.

Meg shook her head.

"I think it was hit deliberately. By a person. While we were . . . busy," he said.

She could tell that Sandy wanted to linger on the new memory of the two of them in the woods. They both excelled at waiting, and, for once, they had stopped waiting. Wrapped in two of his jackets for warmth, comfort, and cover . . .

The metallic taste of guilt rose on her tongue.

No, it was blood. The goose. Of course. There was blood in the air.

Her senses could no longer drift elsewhere; they were

riveted to the bird. She couldn't keep her eyes off it. More than the blood and brains, it was the celebratory flecks of color that disturbed her the most. That wasn't confetti. Shiny and bright, they were bits of photograph. He had been leaving his mark of Kodak everywhere.

"Katie!" Meg shouted, turning toward the house. "Katherine Elizabeth Carroll! Come out here right now." She couldn't say his name. Katie's came flying off her tongue.

"I think it was *him*," Sandy said.

"What do you want?" Katie called from the front door.

"Where is he?"

"Who?" she said.

"Not now, Katie. Where is he?"

"Have you seen him around the house?" Sandy tried. Trying, always, to help.

"Come outside, please," Meg said.

"Yuck!" Katie said, when she saw the bloody mass at their feet.

"Do you know what happened?"

Katie shook her head and muttered yes, then nodded while saying no. A cartoon take of an inept liar. Meg remembered who was in charge.

"Start from the beginning," Meg said. "Just tell me what happened. Just tell the truth. If you tell the truth, no one will get punished." *This, Katie, this is how you lie.*

"We were just playing in the woods," Katie began. "Well, we saw the school bus and we were going to follow you." She changed tacks. "What were *you* doing on the school bus, anyway?"

"Oh, no," Meg said. "You most certainly do not get a question right now."

"I know," Katie said, chagrined. "So we were going to look for you, but we couldn't find you, so we decided maybe we should light some fires."

Meg managed a stern look.

"Everyone's blaming me anyway, so why not?" Katie said. "For your information, we didn't get very far. It was way too wet. But then that goose started coming up to us. I think it wanted food or something. Like we would *feed* it. Isn't it supposed to be a wild goose?"

"How did it end up this bloody mess on our front lawn?"

"He called it over, like a dog or something, and then they started to dance around each other. It was so dumb, it kept not flying away. Like it didn't even know it was in trouble."

So it had become a pet after all, Meg thought.

"Anyone could see by how he picked up a stick that it was in trouble," Katie went on, knocking between fear and disgust. "Then he started swinging the stick, but the stupid goose kept pecking its head towards him. Like it wanted to get its head smashed in. Like it actually wanted to."

Meg recalled the list he had enumerated on the bus, the things in the body that protect you: skin, fat, hair, a very advanced nervous system. Flight, if you're a goose. She pictured him, shot with adrenaline, able to hoist a tree limb as a weapon. But what had happened to the goose's flight instinct?

"Finally," Katie said, "the goose went like this." She put

a toe over an imaginary line. "And he got it. Right in the head."

"By mistake, maybe," Meg tried. "He was playing with it, and—"

"Mom, you didn't see him. He was crazy. Like he wanted to smash it off the face of the earth. I went down to the dingle. I couldn't watch."

"But he's a good boy."

"Not really," Katie said. "Even though you always think so."

Meg changed her mind, hoped instead that one goose *had* been the same goose all the time, for the species' sake. So no more of their flock would be bludgeoned.

Katie kept her toe going, toward the bloody heap of goose.

"Don't," Meg said, grabbing Katie's hand. "It could have diseases."

She squeezed her hand much harder than she should have, until the fingers glowed crimson. She wondered, Can I actually burst my daughter's hands?

"That doesn't hurt, you know," Katie said. "Nothing anyone does hurts."

Pain, Meg could see, was no longer a consequence for Katie. Nor was punishment, nor apology. Not smoke and not fire. Her consequences had already happened. And now, as she'd said, she was trying to make her actions worthy of them.

In Katie's rising humidity, Meg could feel her daughter about to cry. She whispered into her hair, "It's all right. It's all right. I'm right here, honey." *Honey Bear*—that's how Katie'd gotten her nickname.

Katie pulled away and swatted her hair free. But she apologized. "Sorry, Mom, that itches," she said. "I don't really care if you want to hug me. But it made my hair itch."

"Can I ask you something?" Meg ventured.

"You can *ask*. But I can't guarantee that I'll answer."

"Fair enough," Meg said. "Is this your brother?"

"Is that your question?" She set her jaw like her father and spoke through her teeth. "I told you a million times already."

Meg could not remember a single instance. "Tell me a million and one, please."

"Dad thinks it is."

"How about you?"

From her jumpy eyes, her mother could tell she was playing out possibility: *Charlie's such a weakling, how could he have killed something?* She was chewing her lower lip, something she hadn't done since she was little.

"What if I say I don't even care?" Katie said.

"I wouldn't believe you."

In a rare glimpse, Meg saw in her teenager the child who'd once loved the mother and the adult who would again one day.

"I think you do care." She put her hand on Katie's head, and, when Katie didn't pull away, she tucked her daughter's hair behind her ears. "And I think that's good enough. How about that?"

Katie shrugged, confused, relieved, curious. A breeze riffled between them, a pleasant exchange of air. Followed by the nauseating smell of dead fowl.

"Ugh, Sandy," Meg said. "Will you please get rid of that thing?"

"I'm sorry," he said, kneeling by the goose.

"You don't have to *carry* it," she said. "For heaven's sakes, call Animal Control."

"Sorry to start this." He scooped it up, "Got it," and turned to leave.

"Sandy," she called.

He looked back over his shoulder.

"Next time you come over," she said, "please don't bring any more surprises."

He gave her an open-ended look, half smile, half apology. There was a certain inverse proportion at work: two people growing more involved as one walks away.

"Why did he bring that here, like he was giving it to us?" Katie asked once he was gone.

"Good question," Meg said.

"Look." Katie pointed up the street. "The little murderer."

He dashed out of the woods. He appeared to be saluting. No, he was shielding his eyes with his hand, like a voyager who had not seen sunlight in days. When he noticed them, he set off weaving in and out of trees, as if to stitch them to the road.

Meg waved him over, but he ran in the other direction, up the street, legs kicking up behind him like a colt. Or like an eight-year-old boy.

"I don't want to get near him," Katie said. "You never know what else he's going to waste." She tried to scoff, but, judging by how quickly she rushed into the house, Meg could tell that Katie was good and scared.

"What on earth happened?" Meg said. He must have let her catch up, because he certainly could have gotten away if he'd wanted to.

"That goose," she said. "What did you do?"

"Nothing," he said.

"None of that," she said. "No more games. And no more 'nothing.' This is extremely serious. To *kill* something. I don't even know what to say to that."

Because he had been so exceedingly, unnervingly polite all the time, she had vowed to give him a break the first time he did something wrong. But she'd had no idea it would be *this* wrong.

"Is he back because something's the matter?"

"Who?"

He widened his eyes to indicate *You know who.*

"Jeff?" she said.

"And then when it's fixed he'll leave again?"

"I suspect, yes, he will have to go back to Canada at some point. He has a lot of work to do there, and work is very important to him."

"So he's going to leave when everything's back to normal, back to how it used to be?"

"Yes," she said. "I'm afraid he probably will." In fact, she was afraid he probably already had.

"Will *you* leave?" he said.

She remembered that night only from the end, so she could bear it. She pictured the light, which came in streaks at first, as if it didn't dare. Then slashes of noctilucent clouds opened up the sky, and day came pouring into the woods. The night had passed interminably and indistinctly, and when morning came she wasn't entirely convinced that it was a new day. All she knew was that she couldn't very well go home, and yet that was the only thing she could do.

Morning was well under way by the time she did. She did not call his name—silence felt right, the house returned to an original state—but she did make a thorough search, inside and out, even checking the barrel of seeds in the garage. She searched room after room, possible hiding place after possible hiding place. No Charlie . . . and no Charlie . . . and still . . .

He was not lying in his bed, cold and unwakable. Then again, he wouldn't be. Sixty pounds of still, dead weight— no fight and no back talk—he would have made light work for QuicKonnect-dispatched medics.

Or had he in fact passed the night sleeping soundly? *All better now, thank you very much. A little hot in these flannel pajamas, but not so bad when you unsnap the top.* Come morning, no one would have made him eat breakfast of an egg with brewer's yeast, calling it Parmesan cheese, sitting with him, not exactly patiently, but sometimes there was nothing to do except sit with him, as he tried, really tried, but failed in the end to eat enough. Then, with no one there to let him miss school if he wanted, he would have gone outside to board the waiting bus.

Or maybe he decided, for a change, to follow his mother out of the house, down the road, down to the dingle, where now he was hiding with all the beginner's luck in the world.

"Hey," he said, snapping his fingers in front of her face.

She blinked at him, surprised. She couldn't tell if he was being rude, like a teenager, or simply practical, a hypnotist, trying to get her back, to complete what he'd started. "What kind of a way is that to talk to a mother?"

"What if something happened to Charlie?" he said. "If something bad happened to Charlie, you would have to stay, right?"

"If *what* happened?" she dared.

"Don't you know that goose's name?" he said.

"I certainly don't care right now what you've named—"

"Charlie Carroll. That's who that goose was. He was Charlie Carroll." He spoke with the self-conscious precision and slight embarrassment of someone speaking his own full name.

"And now he's dead, you know," he said.

She raised a hand but stopped herself. She had slapped Katie before, on the wrist (nothing minor about an actual slap on the wrist), but never him. Meg wished it were her daughter standing here, having committed a mortal sin. Katie she knew how to get angry at.

But him? He patted his stubbled skull, touched his skinny chest as if checking his parameters. She was looking right at him, but she could not get a fix on him. Each frame split in two: a boy who desperately wanted the goose as a pet, yet his final, loving act was to crack its skull open with a tree branch; a boy who was trying to impress the teenage sister, Meg was sure, but instead left her appalled at the sight of him; a boy who wanted to bring the father home so badly that he himself was willing to disappear; a boy who delivered the mother devastating news of the son—*he's dead, you know*—only once he knew she was not going anywhere.

"Charlie's dead," he repeated. "Isn't that what you wanted?"

She grabbed him. "Never say that." She shook him at the shoulders. Hard. Shaking the word out of him bodily, as she'd shaken the heart, lungs, liver, and kidneys out of Dr. Ireland's child model.

What she also shook out of him was breath. Gasping, eyes wide and watery. It was Charlie's look, a boy betrayed by his own lungs, a boy for whom breathing was not always involuntary.

"Okay, okay, okay," she coaxed. "To seven."

Charlie's breathing exercises: Inhale through the nose, exhale through the mouth. Concentrate. Count to seven as you breathe, in and out in and out in and out in, to seven, then seven, then seven again. Keep him counting in order to keep him breathing.

She saw faint numbers forming on his lips, coaching his lungs.

. . . six . . . seven . . . one . . .

Charlie?

She took the inhaler from her coat pocket—still there!—and held it out like you would offer grain to a horse: let him come to you. He took the inhaler, examined it, and gave it back. But that didn't fool Meg. An asthmatic child is often embarrassed by his paraphernalia and might well disavow it.

She reached around and rubbed his quaking back. "Smooth the feather, smooth the feather," she began.

"What?" he said, after getting himself back into the breathing game. "Why are you looking at me like that?"

"Charlie?" she whispered.

The high afternoon sun caught the stubble on his head in an all-too-familiar copper. Perhaps it was no more than this, a cough, a hue, that separates what you know from what you don't know.

Louder, "Charlie?"

No one could say how Charlie would or would not have grown. It might well have been like this, into an open-faced boy with a smudge of freckles, a ready-to-question squint to his eyes. No one could say how his hair would grow in. These copper-in-the-sun sprouts might well be darker, really, revealing their red only in this particular change-of-season light and, even then, only when you knew the mother, knew there was red hair in the family, and knew to look for it.

"Are you all right now?" she said.

"What if I am?" He rubbed his chest, something another boy might do to wipe his hand clean or to muster a little warmth. Something Charlie had been taught to do in order to feel control over his lungs. To remind himself that they weren't bombs ready to go off, they weren't monsters plotting to strangle him; they were spongy organs inside a bony chest.

"What if I wasn't sick anymore?" he asked. "Ever."

"I know someone who would be glad to hear that." She nodded toward the Dopplering sound of an oncoming Saab in low gear.

"He doesn't know anything."

"Don't say that about your father," she said.

The car came into view. She couldn't tell from here whether it had been fixed. It seemed to be listing to the passenger's side, for what that was worth.

The impossibly slow-moving car concealed from her what Jeff knew or didn't know. Had he been to the mechanic? The sheriff? Out for a drive? To put a deer out of its misery? Was he here to make peace with his children before leaving? Or was he here to spirit them away from her—as he *should*—for a long life with them, a life full of making peace with his children before leaving?

"Are you going to leave and marry Mr. Tadaveski?"

"What kind of a question is that?" she said.

"A good one?" he tried, squinting.

"No," she said. "I'm not going to marry Mr. Tadaveski."

"Are you going to not marry him like you're not married to—?" He pointed at Jeff's car.

"No," she said. "No, I'm going to not marry him at all. Not right now. Nothing right now."

"Because of me? I mean," he added quickly, "because of Charlie?"

"What am I going to do with you?" she said.

Before the rhetorical question could reify the actual question—what *was* she going to do with him?—he was off. At once the messenger and the message, he was running toward the car. To greet it. Or dart in front of it. Dare it, maybe. Or warn it. Would he tell Jeff everything, lay claim to his father? His father, who could call a spade a spade, a son a son, a remission a remission. His father rather than his mother, who half the time felt as if she could pass a hand right through him like a finger through flame, barely sensing the outlines of heat, a phantom marker where feeling should be. The other half the time, she felt flame where there might actually be only the ordinary glow of a child.

He was heading toward the car—which meant the *car* was heading toward *him*.

Which meant a life flashed before her eyes again. The coming together of what she feared and what she witnessed and what she lived with. She saw right through him, his insides in fine working order, excitable muscle cells working just how they should, striated and voluntary, smooth and involuntary. His organs the very model of organs—like those of the child model. Except his were not hard plastic. One false move . . . the mud . . . the grille . . . the hole in the gut . . . the loping off into the woods.

She felt it in her feet again, the overwhelming urge to run.

The grind of a steady driver's brakes sounded like the turning of earth with a spade. An aftermath sound, a fated-to-happen sound.

She did run.

Who could say what Charlie would have looked like as his mother knocked him onto the shoulder of the road, yelling "Careful" and "Stop" and "Right now, young man"?

Who could say whether or not he'd look like this: muddy, for one thing, which along with sun and sprint splashed him with a good deal of color? His nose and the corners of the mouth had sharpened some, his face setting itself for a growth spurt perhaps. Who could say whether Charlie, at this age and stage, would have been knocked off his feet or out of his breath if his mother dared use a little force against her feather of a child, for his own good? *Don't touch him*, she used to say to Jeff, who never did. And now here he was, the father, coming headlong at the son in one of the heaviest cars on the road.

This time, *this time*, Charlie would not play dead. This time he would fight back. He would go down swinging. And he would get up swinging, a fist, a foot, whatever he could leverage against his mother. She let his arms windmill all they wanted. Katie was right: you could hardly feel it when he threw a punch.

But she, Meg, was also right: he could hurt himself this way.

"Charlie," she said, trying to catch an arm or two as it flew by. "Charlie!"

"Don't call me that." He managed to wriggle away from her and closer into her at the same time.

"For Christsakes, what's going on?"

Meg glanced up.

Jeff to the no-need-for-rescue.

He had, it turned out, stopped the car a good twenty-five feet away, safely parallel parked on the side of the road.

"Where've you been?" Meg said. The car had not been

fixed, though it appeared that someone had tried to hammer it out from underneath.

"Maybe he went to look for Charlie."

"Enough, Charlie," Jeff said. "Let's go back home."

Meg let go of the arm she'd caught and nudged him forward. "Go on," she said. "Go with your father." *Quick, quick. Before he disappears.* Didn't this boy know that what Charlie wanted most, besides a dog, was to be with his father?

But he didn't budge. He stiffened his body and stood his ground, the fight in him still palpable in his quivery limbs, in his clenched teeth, in his pulsing temples and slit-mad eyes.

Didn't Charlie know that the new boy didn't stiffen his body, did everything he was asked?

"Come on, Chap," Jeff said, hitting his thigh. "Hop to. Let's help your sister pack for her ski trip. Lots of better things for a big, healthy kid to do than this standing around."

He riveted his heels, his toes, into the mud, trying to take root.

Didn't Charlie know that the boy was not here to take root?

"Enough," Jeff said. "Enough. I can't do this anymore." He headed back to his car.

"Doesn't he know anything?" Charlie said. "Doesn't he even know that Charlie's gone?"

And he was.

He ran right by Jeff, by the car, kept running until he got to the opening in the woods. He ducked in, and the serried trees closed ranks behind him.

Jeff drove the rest of the way home. Meg took her time on foot.

The freshest tire tracks—she thought she could make out the deep and narrow and tready tracks particular to a well-cared-for Saab—kept cutting through the freshest bootprints, a small set and a large. Thank God for the organizing principle of chronology, or these tracks would have the car clipping the child and the adult again and again.

Let Jeff go home and tell Katie she could go on her ski trip. Let him tell himself, no doubt, that he could go back to Canada come Monday.

Let Meg go back to the house to wait for Charlie.

Come dinnertime, let her poke her head out the front door to check for him, and check again, getting ready to call his name when—*wait*—she caught sight of him hopping into the mudroom. Or maybe she wouldn't see him come in, just hear him calling "Mom" from inside the house as she called "Charlie? Charlie!" into the open yard, up the street. Maybe he'd turn it into a game, this near miss, going back outside so that he could walk up to the front door and say, "You don't have to yell so loud. I'm right here."

Acknowledgments

I am enormously grateful to my editor, Amy Scheibe, and my agent, Maria Massie, for helping bring this book to life. And a million thanks to my manuscript readers for their many insights and invaluable support: Christopher Noël, Kate Walbert, Eric Zencey, Lisa Lerner, Matthew Goodman, Joy Nolan, Lisa Burdige, and William Lychack.

About the Author

Deborah Schupack has taught writing and literature at Vermont College, The New School, and Yale University. Her articles and short fiction have appeared in numerous publications, including *The New York Times*, *Gettysburg Review*, and *Fiction*. She lives in New York City.